'You are definitely still in love with her.'

Melissa observed him as she watched him put the baby down in the cot.

'No, I'm not.' He turned and offered her his hand to help her get to her feet. She stumbled and he put an arm around her to steady her. Suddenly she found herself very close to him.

'I'm really not,' he said again.

She wondered if he was trying to convince himself, or her.

She wanted him to kiss her. Her eyes moved to his mouth which seemed too enticing, too close.

'I suppose we should go outside and see what our hosts are doing,' he said dazedly, trying to make himself move away from her.

'I suppose we should.'

He leaned his head closer and touched his lips against hers. The feeling was warm and sensual. Gently he explored her in a way that created a storm of emotion inside. She wanted more; she wa for him to wrap his an let her go.

He's a man of cool sophistication.

He's got pride, power and wealth.

At the top of his corporate ladder, he's
a ruthless businessman—an *expert* lover—
and he's 100 per cent committed to staying single.

He's also responsible
for a BABY!

HIS
BABY

He's sexy, he's successful...
And he's facing up to fatherhood!

THE UNMARRIED FATHER

BY
KATHRYN ROSS

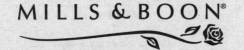

MILLS & BOON®

First published in Great Britain 2000
Harlequin Mills & Boon Limited,
Eton House, 18-24 Paradise Road, Richmond, Surrey TW9 1SR

© Kathryn Ross 2000

ISBN 0 263 82009 2

Set in Times Roman 10½ on 11¼ pt.
01-0008-54113

Printed and bound in Spain
by Litografía Rosés, S.A., Barcelona

CHAPTER ONE

MAC SCHOFIELD sat at his kitchen table and reflected on the fact that he didn't need a woman in his life. He was a single parent, and he was managing just fine. All right, he had the occasional sleepless night, especially recently because Lucy was teething. But he coped with it. Coped with it so well in fact that the company he worked for hadn't realised that there wasn't a Mrs Schofield behind the scenes.

He had been happily unaware of his employer's ignorance concerning his personal circumstances until his contract came up for renewal. Then the misapprehension they were under had suddenly become glaringly obvious.

Mac had been summoned up to J.B. Designs' head office, which was most out of the ordinary. And, even more unusual, he had found himself sitting in the big boss's office, old J.B. himself offering him a cigar and surveying him in that watchful, slightly unnerving way of his.

'How's the family?' J.B. had asked politely.

'Fine, thanks,' Mac had replied, taken aback by the question. In the twelve months Mac had been with the company, J.B. had never had a personal conversation with him—they had only ever discussed work.

He presumed that J.B. had been flicking through his personnel file. What hadn't occurred to him at that juncture was the fact that his personal details had changed since that file had been drawn up.

J.B. had paused. 'You're a talented architect, Mac. We've been very pleased with your work.'

Mac hadn't known whether to be flattered by the compliment, which he knew didn't drop lightly from such a great architect's lips, or to be wary. 'We've been pleased…' sounded as if they might be letting him go.

'As you know, we've only had you here on a short-term contract. The quota of houses you were assigned has now been fulfilled.'

Hell! They were letting him go. Mac's mind had run ahead to his financial commitments, weighing up his situation. Then, in a split second, his pessimistic view of things had been swept away.

'The next major project the company will handle is the design of a new casino in Nevada. I'm looking for someone to head that team.'

Mac had tried to remain nonchalant, but he'd felt a spark of excitement.

'The job won't require a move to Nevada; the company jet will take the team in and out as necessary. Obviously, the person I choose will have to be reliable, exceptionally talented and creative, and able to give one hundred per cent commitment.' J.B. had leaned forward, his bushy eyebrows meeting in the middle as he frowned. 'I haven't decided yet on my top man, but I've been looking through your résumé, Schofield, and I must say, I'm impressed with your work. Would you be interested in the challenge?'

'I certainly would,' Mac had answered without hesitation.

J.B. had nodded as if satisfied. 'Obviously your qualifications and your track record here speak for themselves, but I want to make sure everything else is right, that both professionally and personally I get the right man for the job. To that aim, I'm throwing a cocktail party next week for the candidates that I've short-listed and I'd like you and your wife to come.'

J.B. thought that he was still married. The realisation had floored Mac for a few moments.

It was then that the truth about a few things had suddenly started to come into focus.

J.B.'s reference to having someone at the helm who wasn't afraid of commitment suddenly took on a clarity and meaning that, beforehand, had gone straight over Mac's head. The company's family-friendly policies had also taken on a sharper definition.

Of course, he should have just come straight out with the truth there and then, and told John Bradford in a matter-of-fact tone, Since I applied for the job here and filled out your forms, my wife has left me. I'm a single parent. It wasn't as if his marital status had anything to do with them, anyway. It didn't affect the way he did his work. His life was well-ordered and relatively stress-free. 'Hell, having a woman around full time would probably complicate things anyway,' he muttered out loud now, drumming agitated fingers on the kitchen table. 'They should be relieved that I'm on my own.'

A little shout of impatience made him focus his attention back to the present and to the child who sat beside him in her high chair. 'Well, not completely on my own,' he smiled. 'Sorry, poppet, I was miles away,' he said gently, picking up the spoon to resume feeding her. 'We're doing all right together, aren't we?' he asked as he popped the creamy strawberry dessert into her mouth.

Lucy gurgled through the mouthful of food.

So why didn't I tell the truth? Mac mused to himself. I should have said something like, I don't lack commitment; it was my ex-wife who had that failing. But he hadn't. He had been stunned into silence. Instead, he had thought about how much he liked working for J.B. Designs. He had only been with the company for a year, and already he had risen quite far.

OK, he was a talented architect and if he didn't get his contract renewed he could probably get another job elsewhere, but there was a certain buzz to be had working for such a prestigious firm. They were internationally renowned. He could transfer and work anywhere in the world with them if he ever needed to.

Mac thought about the standard of living he had enjoyed since becoming part of the firm. He had just moved into a luxurious house in one of the most exclusive areas of L.A. He had a shiny red Mercedes which sat on his driveway. And, most important of all, he had a wonderful level of medical insurance cover for himself and any dependents.

All these things had mounted up in his mind when the invitation for him and his 'wife' had been issued, and suddenly Mac had found himself murmuring, 'That would be very nice, thank you.'

Of course, they couldn't deny him a promotion just because he wasn't married, he reasoned sensibly. This was California, home of political correctness. For one thing he could sue them, but that was a bleak prospect compared with the rewards that he could have just by keeping his head down and saying nothing. Mac didn't want litigation, he wanted levitation! He wanted to rise like a brightly shining star within the firm's heavenly portals. Trouble was, as he had listened to J.B., it had become more apparent that being a single father might seriously hinder such progress.

'You do a lot of work from home at the moment,' J.B. had said conversationally. 'You realise that if you get this job you will have to come into the office, here in L.A., most mornings. I take it that isn't a problem?'

'No, of course not,' Mac had said easily. And it wouldn't be. He had an excellent and reliable nanny for Lucy. But somehow even mentioning that fact had suddenly felt like an enormous risk.

'And, as I said before, there will be a bit of travelling backwards and forwards between here and Las Vegas. Will that be a problem with your family commitments?'

'I shouldn't think so. It's just over an hour's flight… Hell, sometimes it takes me that to negotiate the traffic down town.'

It was at that moment Mac had realised just how badly he wanted this opportunity. It wasn't so much the extra money, which would be good. It was more the fact that it would give his creative talents as an architect full rein. He felt he needed to be stretched; he was growing bored with designing office blocks and a few luxury houses. A casino with an almost limitless budget was a chance to be flamboyant, to show what he could really do.

'I can give one hundred per cent,' Mac said, confidently now. 'Can't I, sweetheart?'

Lucy looked up at him as if fascinated by this, her large blue eyes wide with wonder in a face that was framed with a few blonde curls. Mac's heart was overwhelmed with love for the little girl. His daughter…his most precious possession. 'And the more successful I am, the more I can give you.' He bent to kiss her dimpled cheek. She smelt of baby lotion and strawberries. 'Just you and me, kiddo, against the world,' he murmured. 'So what am I going to do about this invitation?'

Lucy gurgled happily.

'You couldn't care less?' Mac said teasingly. 'What kind of caring daughter are you?' He finished spooning the rest of her lunch into her mouth and then carried the empty dishes over to the sink.

As he turned the tap on, he stared out of the kitchen window, still deep in thought. His eyes moved over the churned-up muddy expanse of his garden outside. He was having it professionally landscaped, though at the moment it looked more as if he was having it decimated.

Three men had appeared last week and had dug out all the old concrete. Then no one had appeared for days, and Mac had phoned to complain about the mess and the lack of activity and for it to be put right. Today one person laboured at the far end of what was to be the new patio. It looked as if he was mixing concrete. Mac couldn't see him very clearly because he was some distance away and the heat was shimmering around him, blurring his image. But as he watched he saw him stop work and wipe the back of his hand across his forehead. He'd better go and offer him a cold drink, Mac thought with sympathy. It was no day for hard manual work.

Picking up Lucy and putting her sun bonnet firmly over her curls, he walked outside.

The house was built into the side of the mountain and was on three different levels. It made for stunning views from almost every room out towards the Pacific Ocean. At the moment, though, the view was scarred by the giant muddy crater that used to be his garden. The only areas fit to walk across were the tiled expanse around the empty swimming pool and the wooden deck that led out from the lounge. Mac hoped that he wasn't going to have to put up with this disarray for very long.

He stood by the edge of the swimming pool and shouted to the guy below him. He didn't look round—obviously he couldn't hear over the rumble of the small concrete mixer.

'Excuse me, would you like a drink?' Mac shouted again. The man was bending over with his back to him. He was wearing a peak cap back to front to give protection to his neck from the fierce heat of the midday sun, a white T-shirt, khaki-green trousers and heavy boots.

'Excuse me…' Mac started to shout again. Then, as the machine was abruptly switched off, he found his voice rang clear and unnecessarily loud in the sudden stillness of the air.

'Yes?' The person turned and Mac was astonished to see that the white T-shirt clung tightly to a very shapely figure.

His eyes travelled upwards and met with an arresting

pair of deep-violet-coloured eyes. They were wide and an interesting almond shape with well-defined dark brows. Her skin was clear and fresh. She was probably about twenty-two or three. He couldn't see her hair; it was all tucked up underneath her cap.

'Yes?' she said again, and put a hand on her waist. A very small waist, he noticed, above the baggy trousers.

'Would you like a drink?' From somewhere he pulled his thoughts back.

She smiled, showing an amazing set of perfectly white, even teeth. 'Thanks, I could do with one.'

'Iced tea? Lemonade, Coke?'

'Iced tea would be great.'

'OK, I'll bring it out.' He hesitated. 'Unless you'd like to come inside out of the heat for a while?'

'No. I'm fine out here.' She smiled at Lucy who was watching her with considerable interest. 'Hello,' she said to her softly.

Lucy waved at her.

'You're a beautiful baby,' the woman said, and Lucy suddenly decided to play shy and buried her head into Mac's chest.

'Beautiful but bashful,' Mac said. 'I'll get you that tea.'

The woman smiled and went back to shovelling the concrete mix smoothly over the area that had been marked out.

Mac turned and went back into the house. He felt uncomfortably aware that he wanted to offer to give her a hand. The work she was doing was too back-breaking for one person, especially on a day like today.

Balancing Lucy on his hip, he opened the fridge and took out a jug of iced tea. Then, on impulse, he set two glasses on a tray and went back outside to put them on the table on the wooden deck area. He put up the parasol to shade out the fierce sun and sat Lucy in the high chair he kept for her out there before calling over to the woman.

'You should take a break out of the midday sun for a while,' he said as she walked across towards him.

'I thought you were in a hurry to get the garden finished,' she said with a smile.

'I am.'

As she pulled out a chair and sat down, Lucy reached across and caught hold of her cap, pulling it off her head. Long straight chestnut hair fell in a gleaming silky swathe around her face.

She was stunningly attractive, Mac observed as he watched her laugh at Lucy.

'She's not as bashful as she tried to pretend,' she said as Lucy stuck the cap on top of her sun bonnet, tilted it to an angle and gave a cheeky grin.

'Not nearly,' Mac agreed. He poured two glasses of tea and handed one across to her.

'Thanks.'

'I'm Mac Schofield, by the way, and this is my daughter Lucy.'

She took a sip of her drink. 'Melissa Barnes.'

Her eyes met his across the table. There was a directness about her look, as if she was weighing him up and wasn't trying to hide the fact.

Mac felt disconcerted momentarily. He was a thirty-two-year-old man of the world, confident and not unattractive to members of the opposite sex, yet she made him feel off balance for just a second. Then she lowered her eyes and the sensation passed.

'How old is Lucy?' she asked, turning her attention to the child again.

'Fourteen months.'

'Quite a handful.' Melissa smiled at Lucy, then finished her drink. 'Well, I'd better get back to my work.'

'You could do with some help,' Mac said. 'Are they short-staffed at the garden centre?'

'Yes, they are.' She shrugged her slender shoulders.

'But I'm well able to manage. The path will be finished today, and then I'll position the trellis and obelisks ready for painting. I should be ready to start planting the day after tomorrow.' She fixed him with that direct look again. 'I've looked over the plans that you drew up with my boss, Kurt. There are a couple of queries. For instance, I think your idea to plant clematis against the far gable walls is a mistake; similarly the lonicera nitida shouldn't be placed near the delicate plants on the edge of this patio. It's very fast growing and unless you are prepared to be constantly trimming it and shaping it it will just look a mess.'

Mac frowned. He didn't have a clue what the lonicera nitida was, never mind where it should go. 'I just went along with Kurt's suggestions on most of the planting, as he's the expert—'

'Well, I think we should look at some of the ideas again,' Melissa said decisively. 'Perhaps when your wife is home we could all look at the plans and discuss them. It's important to get the structure of the garden right. Plants are like people, fussy about where they like to live and who their neighbours are.'

Mac smiled at that. 'OK. But you'll have to be content to discuss it with me. The only female of the house is Lucy. My wife is no longer with us.'

'Oh, I'm sorry!' Her soft voice was instantly filled with sincere sympathy.

'Don't be too sorry,' Mac told her easily. 'My wife left me. She's not dead, just divorced.'

'I see.' Melissa stared at him for a moment. Her eyes were an incredible colour, a bluish violet, like the soft petals of a flower. Mac was mesmerised by them. He wondered if she wore coloured contact lenses. Nobody's eyes could be naturally that colour.

'Well, we'll talk about the planting once I get the basic structure of the garden ready. I'll get back to my work. Thanks for the drink, Mr Schofield.'

'You're welcome.' He watched as she took her hat from Lucy and put it on, tucking her hair under it as she stood up. 'And please, call me Mac,' he said.

'Better not.' She smiled politely. 'Kurt likes me to keep a respectful distance from our clients.'

Mac's eyebrows lifted slightly. He wasn't used to a woman being cool towards him. They usually responded very positively. His eyes followed her as she walked away from him. 'An intriguing woman, don't you think, Lucy?' he asked softly.

He wondered if Kurt Patterson was her boyfriend. Then he wondered why he was so interested.

Later in the afternoon, as Lucy was sleeping and Mac was catching up with some paperwork at the kitchen table, the phone rang. It was his mother. Mac sighed inwardly as she got straight to the point. 'I just wondered if you had sorted out what you're going to do about your boss's cocktail party on Saturday?'

'I haven't decided yet.'

'That's so typical of you, Mac,' his mother said with some exasperation. 'It's a few days away and your job rests on it.'

As if he didn't realise that fact! As soon as he had confided his problem to his mother, he had regretted the impulse. The trouble was that Eleanor was all too fond of trying to interfere in his life. She meant well, he was sure, but she had some strange ideas sometimes.

'Now, I think I have the answer for you,' his mother continued briskly.

Mac groaned to himself.

There was a tap at the back door. 'Hold on a moment, Mom,' Mac said, thankful for the interruption. 'Come in,' he called.

'Sorry to interrupt.' Melissa stood in the doorway. 'I've just finished for the day. Do you think I could wash my hands before I go?'

'Certainly.' He waved her towards the sink and then tried to return his attention to his mother.

'I went shopping today,' his mother was saying.

'Uh-huh.' Mac watched as Melissa took off her muddy boots before entering the kitchen. She wore pale pink socks with white daisies on them. He watched as she padded across to the sink. For some reason those pink socks fascinated him.

'I went into that gallery—you know, Jemenio, on Rodeo Drive,' Eleanor continued swiftly. 'And guess who I saw?'

Mac sat up straighter in his chair. 'Mother, I know who you saw. I'd hardly need to be a clairvoyant. Tara Fitzhughes works in that art gallery.'

'Such a lovely girl,' Eleanor gushed. 'She asked to be remembered to you. She's not seeing anyone at the moment, you know.'

'I'm not interested.'

'Don't be like that,' Eleanor said impatiently. 'You should be interested. She's free. That means she could accompany you to the party.'

'What as?'

'Your partner. Don't be obstreperous, Mac. Tara is perfect; she has beauty as well as brains. Plus she is from a very good family. And I know if you explained your circumstances she would readily step into the breach and pass herself off as your wife. It would appeal to her sense of humour.'

'You haven't said anything to her, have you?' Mac grated, irritated beyond words.

'No...but—'

'Good. Don't. The idea is too ludicrous for words, and it's playing with fire. Tara Fitzhughes is looking for commitment. And, far from being amused by your suggestion, she'd be intensely serious about it.'

'What's wrong with that?'

'Everything. It's not fair to her for one thing. I'd rather

pay for an escort to accompany me to the party than get emotionally embroiled with Tara again.'

'Mac!' His mother sounded shocked.

Mac suddenly became aware that Melissa had turned from the sink and was watching him. 'Listen, I've got to go, Mom. I'll speak to you later,' he said hastily.

'My mother,' he explained to Melissa, his tone dry. 'She has a penchant for trying to organise my life.'

Melissa said nothing, just held up her hands. They were wet and he realised she had been looking for a towel, not blatantly listening in.

He got up and handed her one from the rail concealed within the green kitchen units.

'She's trying to get me back with my ex-girlfriend, which is the last thing I want. We only split up a few weeks ago.' He felt as if he needed to clarify things. Though why, he didn't know.

'I wasn't listening,' she said, and then grinned. 'Well, I was trying not to listen.'

Mac turned to put the coffee machine on. 'Trouble is, my boss has invited me to a party at his home on Saturday night and I need a partner to accompany me. Mom saw it as an ideal excuse to get matchmaking.'

'I find it hard to believe that someone like you is short of a date,' she said, crossing the kitchen to put her boots back on.

'It's not exactly a date I'm short of, it's a significant partner in my life.'

She looked up, her hair falling back from her face in a dark, silky flow.

'It's complicated.' Mac shrugged dismissively. 'Suffice to say that my contract is up for renewal at work. Plus there is a promotion in the offing. But I wonder if I'll get either if the firm finds out I'm a single father.'

'That's discrimination,' she said quickly.

'I know. But I'm loath to rock the boat in any way. They think I'm married and I've just gone along with it.'

'So you need someone to pretend to be your wife for one night?'

'Wife or partner. My mother was suggesting I ask my ex-girlfriend.'

'What about asking your ex-wife?'

Mac hesitated. 'I considered the option briefly, but I think it would be treading over dangerous ground.'

'Oh.' Melissa pushed her second foot into her boot and wondered what emotion lay behind those words. She straightened to look at him. 'I'll do it, if you want.'

'You?' He was totally taken aback.

She shrugged. 'Yes. How much will you pay me?'

He stared at her.

'You need a partner. I could use the extra cash.' She sounded completely matter-of-fact.

Mac recovered his equilibrium and grinned. 'This afternoon you wouldn't call me by my first name. You said your boss would object. Now you are offering to pass yourself off as my wife. What would Kurt say about that?'

She glanced at the kitchen clock. 'It's after five. I'd say it has nothing to do with Kurt.'

Mac's eyes moved over her face, the clear healthy complexion, the luminous sparkle of her eyes. 'So how much do you want me to pay you?' he found himself asking softly.

She shrugged. 'How many hours will the party last?'

'I've no idea. But I have no intention of staying late.'

She thought for a moment. 'OK, I'll do it for double my day's salary.'

'How much is that?' he asked with a frown.

She told him.

'You've got yourself a deal,' he said quietly, and at the same time he was wondering at his sanity. This had to be the most bizarre business arrangement ever.

She nodded. 'Just as long as it's understood that you are paying for my company…nothing else.'

His eyebrows rose at that. 'I never for one moment thought about anything else,' he assured her coolly.

'Good,' she smiled. 'See you in the morning, then, Mr Schofield.'

The back door closed behind her before he could say anything else.

CHAPTER TWO

MELISSA was painting the trellis a bright blue. There was something satisfying about it, relaxing almost. But maybe that was because Mac Schofield wasn't at home. She had lost almost a whole night's sleep worrying about facing him again today. It had been such a relief to arrive this morning and find his car gone.

A woman had come out into the garden and introduced herself as Patricia, Lucy's nanny. She'd informed her that Mr Schofield was at the office today, but that if she wanted anything at all she only had to come up to the kitchen.

Melissa had felt transformed by the news, as if she'd had a reprieve from a death sentence. She hummed to herself now as she sat back and surveyed her handiwork.

When she did see Mac Schofield again, she would tell him she had changed her mind about escorting him to his party. She couldn't possibly do anything like that. The very suggestion had been totally out of character.

What kind of madness had descended on her yesterday in Mac Schofield's kitchen? she asked herself furiously.

Then, through the emphatic reasoning as to why she was not going to go through with the idea of escorting Mac Schofield to his damn party, a picture of her mother arose suddenly in her mind.

'I'm fine,' she had assured Melissa when they had spoken on the phone. But Melissa had known that she wasn't being honest.

The truth was that her mother was anything but fine. She was in need of a hip replacement operation. And, according to Melissa's aunt who shared a house with her in Florida, her walking was getting worse and she was obviously in a lot of pain. But she had no medical insurance cover and not enough savings to pay to go into a private hospital. So she was trying to pretend that she didn't have a problem, trying to deny the fact that she was one very frightened woman.

It was this problem that had prompted Melissa into selling her share in the garden design business to her partner, Kurt. She hadn't wanted to sell. She had dedicated three years of her life to building up the business and it was just starting to make some money. However, she needed to help her mother and, as she couldn't raise the money at the bank, selling had been her only alternative. Kurt had been overjoyed to buy her out and had offered her a job with a good salary. So she couldn't complain. Except that, although she had raised enough for her mother's operation, she hadn't got enough for the aftercare she would need.

Yesterday she had been toying with the idea of getting a second job in the evenings. So when she had overheard Mac Schofield on the phone she had thought, Why not? It was a step forward and it all helped.

Only when she had gone home and thought about it had she remembered the look of surprise on Schofield's face. She realised he had been astonished by her suggestion and it was then that apprehension and astonishment had hit. It was just so out of character for her to have said something like that. What Mac Schofield had thought, Lord alone only knew! Maybe she should explain to him that she hadn't been thinking very clearly yesterday, that she was so worried about her mother that she was grasping at any straws.

The sound of a door closing at the house made her jump nervously. She sat back on her heels and looked up towards the building, wondering if it was Mac and, if so, what she should say to him. A couple of minutes later she saw Patricia walking around the side of the house, pushing

Lucy in her pram. She gave a cheerful wave to Melissa. 'See you later,' she called.

Melissa waved back, relieved. She liked Lucy's nanny—a bright, friendly woman of about fifty. Melissa returned her attention to the trellis. She wouldn't worry about Mac Schofield. She'd just tell him she'd changed her mind. He'd find some other woman to step into the breach. After all, he was a very good-looking man.

Melissa hummed a tune to herself as she smoothed paint over the wood. She would put everything out of her head and just think about the garden, she told herself briskly.

A few moments later a shadow fell over her handiwork and she looked up in surprise.

'Hi,' Mac said with a grin. 'How's it going?'

'Very well.' Melissa hoped she sounded composed; she certainly didn't feel it.

Yesterday, Mac Schofield had been casually dressed in chinos and a T-shirt. Today he wore a dark suit, white shirt and colourful tie. He looked every inch the successful businessman. He also looked incredibly sexy. By contrast, Melissa was suddenly very aware of her disarray. She was wearing denim shorts today, and a yellow T-shirt. On her feet she wore thick-soled, lace-up ankle boots.

She hastily put down her paintbrush and stood up to face him, hoping that would restore to her some confidence and poise.

Her eyes met with his and she felt her heart drumming unevenly against her chest. Calm self-assurance seemed to have deserted her.

He had dark, 'come to bed' eyes, dark, thick hair that was stylishly cut, and a body that was powerfully well-honed. Broad and tall, he gave the impression of power. He also oozed the kind of sexual magnetism that was hard to pretend you didn't notice. He should have had the word 'danger' stamped on his forehead, Melissa thought hazily as she gazed into his eyes.

'You startled me,' she said, trying to cover her awkwardness. 'I didn't hear your car.'

'I parked it round the front.' His eyes moved down over her body. It was just a swift, assessing gaze, but it made Melissa feel as if she was naked.

'Do you think I could have a word with you, up at the house?' Mac asked.

Before she could say yes or no, or ask anything, he had turned and was leading the way up towards the back door.

'If it's about what I said yesterday—' she started to say as she hurried after him.

'No, it's about where I want you to plant the bougainvillea.' He looked round at her and grinned as he saw the look of surprise on her face. 'Of course it's about yesterday.' He wiped his shiny black shoes on the back doormat before leading the way into the kitchen.

The cool, air-conditioned room was a welcome balm after the intense heat outside. 'Whew, that's better!' Mac loosened his tie, then pulled it off. 'Can I get you a drink?' He put his briefcase down, then opened the fridge.

'No, thanks, I'd better not delay. I've got a lot of work to get through.'

He glanced around at her. She was standing just inside the door as if poised for flight.

'Have you had any lunch?' he asked suddenly.

'I don't eat much in the middle of the day…'

'You're still entitled to a lunch break. Please stay and have a sandwich with me.' He pulled out a chair for her.

Melissa was tempted for a moment. Then she shook her head. 'Thanks anyway,' she said. Then, taking a deep breath, she continued, 'Listen, about what I said yesterday…accompanying you to that party.'

'Yes?' He was pouring ice-cold lemonade out of a pitcher from the fridge into a long, frosted glass. The sight of it made Melissa feel incredibly thirsty.

'The thing is…I've changed my mind,' she said quickly.

'I don't know what I was thinking of yesterday. It was a mad idea.'

'I'm sorry you feel that way,' he said easily. 'I spent last night thinking what a good idea it was.'

'Did you?' She stared at him incredulously.

'Yes.' He met her eyes directly. 'But if you don't want to do it that's fine. At least sit down and have a drink.'

She hesitated, then smiled. 'OK, thanks.' She took off her gloves and bent down and unlaced her boots, removing them before walking onto the pristine polished wooden floor.

He put the drinks down on the glass-topped table as she sat, then went about making himself a sandwich. The situation was so normal and relaxed that Melissa started to feel the tension that had been coiled tightly inside her subside.

'I've had a hell of a morning at work,' he told her as if he had known her for ever. 'Made me wonder why I want this damn promotion anyway. If I got it, it would mean even more time at the office.'

'And less time with Lucy?' Melissa suggested quietly, sipping her drink.

'Not exactly.' He shrugged. 'Working from home means you have to be disciplined. I have to lock myself away in my studio for the required amount of hours.'

'It must be hard having a baby and a demanding job.'

'Sometimes it is,' Mac conceded. 'But I'm lucky. I've got good back-up with Patricia. She's an old family friend. I've known her and her children for years. Plus my mother helps out as well.'

'When she's not trying to run your life?' Melissa teased.

He laughed. 'Yes, you've got it.'

Melissa wondered where his wife was. It was somewhat unusual for a man to get custody of his child.

He put a platter of sandwiches and two plates down on the table before taking a seat opposite. 'The problem with my mother is that she's desperate for me to get married again. I know she means well, but all that matchmaking starts to grate after a while.'

He picked up the plate of sandwiches and offered her one. After a moment's hesitation she accepted. She was feeling a bit hungry, she realised.

'She was on the phone again last night reminding me of Tara's suitability.' Mac looked glum for a moment. 'Are you sure I can't talk you into coming with me on Saturday?' he asked suddenly. 'You don't need to actually say you're my wife, you know. I'll just introduce you as my partner; it's the same thing.'

Melissa shook her head. 'I don't feel comfortable with the idea.'

'You seemed to yesterday.'

'Well…yesterday I wasn't thinking very clearly.'

'So what were you thinking about yesterday?' he asked.

Melissa hesitated. 'I was worrying about my mother.' She took a sip of her lemonade and felt its icy cold fingers permeating down through her body. 'She isn't very well at the moment.'

'What's wrong with her?'

'She fell last year and badly damaged her hip. She's only fifty-eight, and was very fit and active before. Now she has difficulty managing the small front step at her house.' Melissa put her glass down and ran her hand in a distracted way over her dark hair as she leaned back in her chair. 'I know she needs an operation, which is fine. I've managed to get enough money together in order to book her into one of the best private hospitals. It's the aftercare that's holding things back. She's going to need several weeks, if not months, of constant care. I can't afford to give up my job and go and look after her myself—I wish I could. Yesterday I was considering getting myself an evening job.'

'And I was a first step?'

'You were a moment of insanity,' Melissa said with a wry twist of her lips. 'I was feeling a bit desperate.'

'Thanks!' He grinned. 'So why have you changed your mind?'

'I think I need something a little more steady,' she said with a smile. 'Bar work, or waitressing. Bogus wife hardly fits the job description.'

He laughed. 'It's different, I'll grant you that. Have you been to see about another job?'

She shook her head. 'Not yet.'

'So meanwhile Saturday night is free?'

'Well…'

'I'll pay double what we agreed yesterday,' he offered before she could turn him down again.

The offer surprised her. 'I thought you had changed your mind about the job being important to you?' she countered.

'Did I say that?' He met her eyes and then smiled. 'Maybe it was a fleeting feeling.'

When he smiled at her like that she felt her body reacting to him in a very positive way. Mac Schofield had a charisma that was sexually sizzling. Melissa had never known anything like it. She could feel a tingling awareness of him right down to her toes. She wondered if he was conscious of the power of his looks, of his smile. Her eyes moved over the determined line of his square jaw, his dark eyes, the firm set of his lips. It might be fun to pretend to be his partner for an evening.

'I'll tell you what,' she said impulsively. 'I'll do it for you, but you don't need to pay me.'

Now it was his turn to look surprised.

'Call it a favour from one person with mother trouble to another.'

Before Mac could answer her there was a noise from the front of the house and a woman's voice called out Mac's name.

'Speak of the devil.' Mac grinned at her.

Melissa smiled back at him. 'I'd better get back to work,' she said, getting up from the table. 'Thank you for lunch.'

'It wasn't much.' Mac stood up. 'How about having dinner with me tomorrow night?'

The invitation was sudden and for a second Melissa wasn't sure if he was asking her out on a date.

'We should get to know each other a little better before we try to pass ourselves off as a couple, don't you think?' Mac continued swiftly. 'After all, you don't even know what I do for a living, do you?'

'Actually, I do. Kurt told me you were an architect,' she admitted.

'Well, even so, I'd like to know more about you.' His voice was gently persuasive.

He was being practical, Melissa reminded herself. He could hardly pass her off as his partner if he didn't know the first thing about her, and vice versa. Yet there was something about the way he held her eyes that made her heart miss a beat.

'I won't ask Patricia to babysit because she will be doing that the night after when we go to the party. But how about if you come over here, around seven-thirty? I'll cook something for us.'

She smiled. 'That would be nice. Thank you.'

'Mac?' A door slammed in the hallway and the next moment his mother walked into the room.

'Oh, I'm sorry,' the woman said, stopping in surprise. 'I didn't realise you had company.'

'It's all right, Mother. You're just in time to meet Melissa before she gets back to work. Melissa, this is my mother, Eleanor.'

Melissa smiled politely at the woman. She was about sixty, with light blonde hair, very attractive, slim, and elegantly dressed in a cream trouser suit. She made Melissa acutely conscious of her state of dress.

'I'm working on the garden,' Melissa said.

Eleanor smiled. 'Well, it's nice to meet you, dear,' she said briskly.

'And you.' Melissa nodded and headed for the door.

'Speak to you later, Melissa,' Mac called after her. 'Don't hesitate to come in if you need anything.'

Melissa picked up her shoes and gloves from the door and stepped out into the back porch to put them on.

'What are you going to do about Saturday?' she heard Eleanor saying. 'Because Tara won't be available if you don't get a move on, Mac. She's an attractive girl and—'

'It's all right, I'm all fixed up for Saturday,' Mac cut across her easily.

'Oh?' There was wariness in his mother's tone. 'You've rung Tara, then?'

'No. Melissa is going to accompany me.'

'Melissa?' His mother sounded astounded. 'Melissa who?'

'You just met her,' Mac said impatiently.

'You mean that pretty girl who is doing the garden?'

'That's right.'

'I see…' The fire died in his mother's voice. 'She seems very nice. Is her family from around here?'

'Don't start, Mom. It's a pretence…she's doing me a favour, no strings attached.'

The note of finality in Mac's voice was obviously not one to be argued with. He'd let his mother go so far but no further. She fell silent.

Melissa moved away guiltily, aware that she had lingered longer than she should.

CHAPTER THREE

MELISSA parked her car next to Mac's on the drive and got out. It was a warm evening. No hint of a breeze stirred the tall poplars that screened the front of the house. There was an airless muggy feeling as if a storm was approaching.

Security lights flooded over her as she walked towards the front door and rang the doorbell. Some wisteria would look lovely growing up the front of this house, she thought as she waited. And perhaps some terracotta plant pots at the edge of the brick drive. She'd suggest it to Mac over dinner. In fact, if she could stick to talking about the garden, it would probably be a lot easier to get through the evening.

She felt a bit awkward about this situation. It wasn't a date. Yet it wasn't strictly business either. She wondered if the real problem was the fact that she found Mac Schofield sexually attractive. He made her very aware of herself as a woman—a detail reflected in the fact that it had taken her ages to decide what to wear tonight. The last person who had made her feel like that was Simon. And Simon had broken her heart.

The door swung open, interrupting her thoughts.

'Hi.' Mac smiled at her, and she felt her heart starting to beat in an irregular and most discomfiting way. 'Come on in.'

He was dressed very casually in jeans and a light blue T-shirt. She was immediately glad that she had resisted the impulse to get dressed up tonight.

She had reminded herself that she was dining in Mac's house and, anyway, she didn't have to try and prove herself—it wasn't as if Mac was interested in her personally. So she had selected a long black skirt and teamed it with a white scooped-neck silk top and flat shoes. It was smart yet casual. Her hair was loose and it gleamed under the light as she stepped into his hall.

'You'll have to forgive me, but I'm running a bit late,' he said as he led the way through the house towards the lounge. 'Lucy has been playing me up. Maybe she's just teething again, but she has been very cranky. Most unlike her usual sunny-natured self.'

'Is there anything I can do to help?' Melissa offered.

He turned and smiled warmly at her. 'No, but thanks for offering. I've got her settled now and dinner is under control.'

Melissa tried not to notice how attractive he was, how his smile lit his eyes. Instead she dragged her eyes away from his tall, well-built body and concentrated on the decor of the house. She had only ever seen the kitchen before, but the rest of the house was equally impressive and very modern in design. The hallway was large and airy with a staircase that curved gracefully up to a minstrel gallery above.

The lounge looked like a picture from one of the glossy home magazines that Melissa subscribed to, yet it had a lived-in, comfortable look. Squashy soft settees in buttery gold shades against the terracotta carpets gave it a warmth that Melissa immediately liked. Fine muslin curtains edged in gold decorated enormous sliding doors which led out to the deck.

'You have a lovely home,' she said, taking the seat that he waved her towards. 'I'll have to ensure that I make the outside as perfect as the decor inside.'

'I'm sure you will.'

There was a moment's awkward silence as their eyes met across the room. 'You look very nice, by the way,' he said politely, his eyes moving over her appearance. She wondered if he was being kind. Mac Schofield probably only dated very glamorous women. A picture rose in her mind of a beautiful blonde with long hair and long, long legs. That would be the type of woman Mac Schofield would be attracted to. She forced a smile to her lips and accepted the compliment gracefully.

'What would you like to drink?' Mac asked.

'A glass of white Zinfandel, if you've got it?'

He nodded. 'I won't be a moment.'

As she waited, she got up and looked at the photographs that lined the mantelpiece. They were all of Lucy, from newborn to present day.

'I could be accused of being a little bit boring where my daughter is concerned,' Mac said as he came back into the room and saw her studying them. 'My photos are all a case of baby by the door, baby by the swing, baby by the chair.'

'I think it's lovely that you're such a devoted dad,' Melissa said honestly as she turned and accepted the glass of wine from him.

She wondered how tall he was. Standing this close to him, she noticed that she had to tip her head right back to look into his eyes. Probably about six-four, she guessed.

'Your boyfriend didn't mind you coming here tonight, I take it?' he asked suddenly.

The question really threw her off balance. 'Boyfriend?'

'Kurt? I got the impression that he might be a bit more than just your boss.'

'Heavens, no.' She took a hasty sip of wine. She had dated Kurt once—he was a lovely guy—but they hadn't had much in common except a love of gardening. She would probably never have accepted his invitation except that she had been so lonely at the time. It had been just after she had split up from her fiancé.

'Kurt and I were business partners once,' she explained

to Mac, 'but I recently sold my share of the garden centre to him, so now he's just my employer.'

'I see.' Mac's eyes moved over her face searchingly. 'It must be difficult working for someone when you used to be equal partners.'

'Yes…' Melissa sighed '…it is. I invested a large amount of time and energy towards the business. Now I have to take a back seat and it's hard. I find myself having to bite my tongue when Kurt does something that I would never have agreed to.'

'Did you sell out to him because of this problem of your mother's health?'

Melissa hesitated. 'Well, partly,' she admitted cautiously.

'I'm sorry,' Mac said gently. 'That's really tough.'

The warmth in his voice flowed through her senses, creating a heat that had nothing to do with the social pleasantries of the conversation.

'It's not so bad.' Melissa smiled. 'At least I've still got a good job. And I enjoy it for the majority of the time.'

'So, there's no boyfriend, then?' Mac asked casually.

'Not at the moment, no.' She tried to sound nonchalant, but deep down she was more than a little bit pleased that he was asking.

'I'm glad.' Mac took a sip of his drink.

She looked up at him questioningly, wondering if he was making a pass at her.

'Well…it's one less complication, isn't it?' Mac grinned. 'I'd have hated for some guy to appear at my boss's party on Saturday night, punch me on the nose, and accuse me of stealing his girl.'

'I don't suppose it would impress your boss very much,' Melissa agreed, trying not to feel disappointed.

'No, I don't suppose it would.'

His eyes moved over her. They were gentle and assessing, and yet disturbing beyond reason. 'I can't believe my luck that you're free tomorrow night.'

'Well, I'm sure that if I hadn't stepped into the breach someone else would have.'

'Maybe. But I'm glad I've got you,' Mac said with a smile.

Hell, but he was smooth, Melissa thought, trying very hard to ignore the sensual chaos he was wreaking on her senses. She reminded herself of what he'd said to his mother. 'It's a pretence…she's doing me a favour…' That was all this was.

'Your mother wasn't too disappointed that you hadn't contacted your ex-girlfriend, then?'

'No, I think she understood…finally.' Mac took a sip of his wine. 'I mean, there's nothing wrong with Tara *per se*. In fact she's a nice girl, but we have nothing in common. That's why I ended our relationship. Although we are still on friendly terms, I couldn't ask her to accompany me to this party—it would be deeply unfair to her, plus deeply uncomfortable for me.'

'Yes, I see.' Melissa paused. 'And you couldn't ask your ex-wife?' She couldn't help herself questioning him again on that subject. She was intrigued to know what kind of a man he was, what had happened to his marriage.

'No. Kay is seeing someone at the moment anyway.' He changed the subject swiftly. 'What about you, Melissa? Have you ever been married?'

She shook her head. 'Engaged once. But it didn't work out.'

'What happened?'

She shrugged. 'Two weeks before our wedding I discovered my fiancé, Simon, had been cheating on me with someone I thought was my best friend.' It was strange how easy it was to tell him that. She hadn't meant to. It was something she never talked about as a rule, something she didn't like talking about.

Mac grimaced. 'By the sound of it, you probably had a very lucky escape.'

'Yes. It didn't feel like it at the time, though.' Melissa looked down at her drink. In truth it had felt like the end of the world—she had really loved Simon.

'How long ago was that?'

'About a year.' It would be a year next weekend. She knew the date exactly. It was hard to forget. Everything had been organised for their wedding. Her white dress had hung in her bedroom, the invitations already sent out. She switched her thoughts abruptly away from that. 'How long is it since your divorce?'

'The same. About a year.'

Melissa waited to see if he would tell her what had happened. He didn't, so she didn't ask. Instead she said, 'It must have been a very difficult time, especially with Lucy being so young.'

'It wasn't easy.' His lips twisted ruefully. 'I didn't know the first thing about looking after a new baby. I put diapers on back to front. It took me an hour just to dress her in the mornings. She was so tiny…so fragile. I was terrified of her.'

It was hard to imagine a big strong man being frightened of a baby. Yet Melissa understood what he meant. 'The feeling of responsibility must have been overwhelming,' she said softly.

'Yes, it was.' His eyes held hers for a moment. 'I'll never forget the moment when she was first put into my arms at the hospital. The enormity of knowing that I helped bring this child into the world and the knowledge that it was down to me to make sure I got everything right for her…' He shook his head. 'It was awesome.'

'Were you and your ex-wife still together at that point?'

Mac shook his head. 'Kay had decided she wanted a divorce a month before Lucy was born.' He frowned suddenly. 'But I don't want to bore you with all that. Let's go through to the dining room and eat, shall we? Hopefully I haven't burnt everything.'

Melissa would have liked to tell him he wasn't boring her. On the contrary, she was curious to know more, but she sensed he didn't really want to talk about it and she could understand that.

So she followed him through to the dining room and sat at the table. It was beautifully laid—silver set against snowy white linen and white candles adorning the centre. On the sideboard there was a large vase of fresh white lilies, their glossy green leaves and fragrant perfume setting off the effect perfectly.

'You've gone to a lot of trouble,' Melissa said as he placed the starter of smoked salmon in front of her. 'I'm surprised you've had the time, with Lucy not being so well tonight.'

Mac grinned as he sat opposite. 'It's my appearance that has suffered as a consequence of Lucy's tears. I haven't had time to change.'

'You didn't need to change for me anyway,' she said. 'You look good the way you are.'

As soon as she said that she wished she hadn't: it sounded too personal somehow.

'Thanks.' She could hear amusement in his tone and wondered what he was thinking. She didn't dare look over at him but instead concentrated on the delicious food in front of her.

'Anyway, I'm here for you to tell me all about this party tomorrow night,' she continued swiftly. 'Not for you to impress me.'

'But I wouldn't mind impressing you a little,' he said quietly. 'I do have my male vanity to consider.'

She glanced over at him, saw the teasing light in his dark eyes, and smiled.

How could his wife ever bear to leave him? she found

herself wondering. He seemed so decent, so warm. Maybe he had been a womaniser?

Realising that she had probably held his eyes longer than she should, she glanced away. 'Well, pandering to your male ego, I should tell you that dinner is delicious,' she said softly.

'Thanks. I like cooking, although I don't get much time to do a lot.'

'Neither do I,' Melissa admitted. 'But I'm not a wonderful cook. I tend to incinerate most things.'

Mac laughed. 'Well, if you ever invite me over to your place remind me to arrive with a take-away.'

It was just a joking, casual remark, but it made Melissa's heart miss a tiny beat. It made her think how pleasant it would be to open her front door and see him standing on her porch, calling for her...on a date...leaning forward to kiss her.

She reached for her wine and told herself very fiercely to stop thinking like that. What the hell was the matter with her?

While she was trying to pull her thoughts back together, she realised the conversation had moved on. Mac was telling her about his boss—the mighty J.B., he called him. Melissa tried to concentrate.

Her eyes moved over his face. Lean, well-defined cheekbones, square jaw. There was a very sensuous look about Mac Schofield, an air of dangerous excitement. Maybe it was his well-honed body, maybe the arrogant male gleam in those eyes, but you knew just by talking to him for two minutes that here was a man who could have it all. A man who had never been afraid of life, a go-getter, a high achiever, not averse to taking a few risks. Yet that charisma was tempered with something else. An air of stability. Maybe it was the fact that he seemed such a caring parent.

He glanced over and caught her watching him. 'So, what do you think?'

The question made her realise she had only been half listening. She reached for her glass again and chose her words carefully. 'I was wondering how your boss got the impression that you are still married?'

'I don't know.' He shrugged. 'It must have been on my résumé when I first applied for a job with the company. That was before Lucy was born and before Kay had left. By the time I'd got through the last of the interviews and been told the job was mine, Kay was filing for divorce.'

'But you never mentioned it?'

'It wasn't an intentional omission. I work mostly from home. At the office I talk shop. I suppose when I mention my home life I talk about Lucy.'

'And maybe you hoped that your wife would come back to you?' Melissa suggested softly.

'You mean I was in denial?' His lips twisted ruefully. 'Perhaps I was, for a while. But I wasn't aware of the misapprehension that J.B. was under until he called me into his office and told me there was a chance they might keep me on, plus give me a promotion.'

'What do you think your chances are of getting it?'

'Not bad. Four other people have been short-listed.'

'And are they all married?'

'The three men are all married with families, the fourth is a woman. She's got no children and is living with her partner, from what I gather.'

'Maybe you're just imagining that your boss is stuck in the Dark Ages. It probably doesn't matter a jot that you're a single parent. All that counts is that you are good at your job.'

'I'd like to believe that.'

'But you don't?'

'Not from the way J.B. has been talking recently. This is an enormous project. If I get the job, my first task will be heading a design team to create one of the world's largest casinos in Las Vegas.'

Melissa's eyebrows rose. 'Will that mean you'll be moving to Nevada?'

He shook his head. 'The company jet will be whisking me backwards and forwards whenever necessary.' He grinned. 'In fact we've all joked that it will probably be quicker to get out there than it is to get to the office some days.'

'Sounds exciting.'

'Yes. But I believe if J.B. knows I'm a lone parent it's going to raise some doubt in his mind about my level of commitment. He's very edgy about the project as it is. There's mega money at stake.'

'And do you have any doubts about the amount of time you will be able to commit?' Melissa asked quietly.

'No, of course not. I wouldn't even contemplate it if I did.' He frowned, as if her words had disturbed him for a second. Then he shook his head. 'My life with Lucy runs very smoothly. There is no reason why I can't take on a bigger project and more responsibility.'

He got up to clear the plates away and serve the main course. The conversation drifted away from his work. They talked about nothing in particular for a while: living in California, the weather, the earth tremor last week. They were very much on the same wavelength on certain things, Melissa noticed. And they shared a similar sense of humour.

'How did you get into gardening?' Mac asked her, leaning across to refresh her glass with some sparkling water.

'I've always been interested in plants, even as a child. There is something totally satisfying about growing things, nurturing them, watching nature in all its glory.'

'So it's more of a passion than a mere job?'

'Definitely.' She smiled. 'I'm very passionate about

plants. I studied horticulture at university for a few years, then worked with a garden designer called Simon Wesley.'

She paused for a moment, thinking about Simon, about their relationship. 'He's very talented; he's designed gardens for the rich and famous of Beverly Hills.' She forced herself to continue as if she were talking about someone who had meant nothing, just a well-liked boss...not a lover, a man she had planned to spend her life with. 'Now he has his own TV gardening programme.'

'Yes, I've heard of him. In fact the company I work for has consulted him from time to time,' Mac said, looking impressed. 'My garden is obviously in very capable hands.'

Melissa smiled. 'It will look fantastic when I've finished with it. A positive picture of loveliness.'

Mac stared at her across the table. She was a positive picture of loveliness, he thought suddenly. He liked the sparkle of vitality in her eyes, the dark satin texture of her hair against the honey blush of her skin, the way the silk top she wore had a sheen that glimmered in the candle-light, highlighting the soft swell of a voluptuous, decidedly feminine figure. He thought suddenly that he would like to take her to bed, taste the softness of her lips, breathe in that delicate, flowery perfume.

Silence had fallen between them. Her eyes were locked on his.

Melissa felt an inexplicable sense of anticipation, so intense, so perturbing that it made her almost breathless. She couldn't understand the feeling. She tried to dismiss it as a figment of her imagination.

It was almost a relief when the sound of Lucy crying interrupted the silence.

'I thought the peace and tranquillity of the house was too good to be true,' Mac said, pushing back his chair.

'I'll clear the table while you see to her,' Melissa said, also standing up.

'There's no need...'

'I don't mind,' Melissa assured him briskly. 'Then I should really be making tracks.' She tried to sound sensible, tried to dismiss the feelings that had sprung to life a few moments ago.

Mac paused at the doorway and looked around at her. 'Don't go,' he said. 'Stay and have some coffee with me.'

She hesitated, and Lucy's cries intensified from upstairs. 'And if you'd make the coffee, all the better?' he asked with a raised eyebrow.

She smiled. 'You've got yourself a deal.'

Mac nodded. 'Better go. I won't be long.'

Despite the words, Mac was upstairs some time. Melissa had loaded the dishwasher and brought a tray of coffee through to the lounge and he still wasn't back.

She put the tray down on the table and walked to the patio doors, sliding them back to stare out at the night. A warm breeze had sprung up; it was coming straight in from the sea. Melissa could hear the distant sound of the waves breaking against the shoreline and far out into the darkness a flash of lightning lit the sky. It illuminated the inky black Pacific as if someone were switching a light bulb on and off.

As she watched the gathering storm she thought about dinner and wondered if she had imagined the way Mac had looked at her. She was almost certain that desire had lit the darkness of his eyes, and it had set an immediate answering clamour alive inside her. The feelings excited her, but they also scared her. She hardly knew Mac Schofield, and yet he stirred up so many strong emotions within her. Every female instinct told her that she would welcome his kiss, the passion of his embrace. Yet there was another voice inside her urging caution and reminding her what it felt like to be hurt by a man who held such power over your senses.

'Seems like there's a storm approaching,' Mac said from behind her, making her jump.

She turned and looked at him across the room and felt her heart thundering against her chest. At the same time a loud crash of thunder split the air and it started to rain. Enormous drops of water bounced on the wooden decking outside, making a musical drumming sound.

Melissa wrenched her eyes away from his. 'Yes, I'd better close this door.' She turned and pulled at the heavy frame, aware at the same time that he was crossing behind her to help.

'Here, let me.' He reached across her from behind. She felt his body close to hers, the brush of his arm as it went around her to glide the door smoothly back into place.

The sound of the storm was muffled now. Yet the storm inside Melissa seemed to have increased dramatically. She turned as he stepped back. 'How is Lucy?'

'She's gone back to sleep.' His eyes moved over her face. She wondered if he knew how the slight touch of his body had stirred her senses.

There was another boom of thunder outside.

'Though if this keeps up I don't suppose she will be for long.'

'No, I don't suppose she will.' Melissa made a pretence of looking at her watch. 'I should go, Mac. It's getting late and—'

'You can't go out in this weather.' He frowned. 'Besides, you haven't had your coffee yet and we haven't discussed the details of tomorrow night.'

The rain was driving against the windows like the insistent tapping of thousands of tiny fingers clamouring to get in.

'What details?' She watched as he sat on the settee and started to pour the coffee.

'Little things like how long we have been together, that

kind of thing. If people ask we can't be giving different answers, can we?'

'I suppose not.' Melissa went to take a seat opposite him.

'I was thinking that it's probably best if we stick to the truth as much as possible.' He handed her the coffee cup. 'I'll introduce you as my partner. Then if the subject of Lucy comes up we'll make it clear that she is my daughter by my first marriage. Does that sound OK to you?'

She shrugged. Now that they were down to the basic mechanics of deception, she wasn't so sure about this.

'Are you having second thoughts?' he asked suddenly.

'No.' She hesitated. 'It's just that I'm not completely sure I'll be able to carry it off.'

'Of course you will. You'll be perfect.'

There was another growl of thunder outside accompanied by the sound of Lucy crying.

Mac shook his head. 'I'm sorry about this. It's not like Lucy at all.'

'It's OK, you go and see to her. I'll really have to go now.' She finished her coffee and stood up. 'I think we've just about covered everything anyway.'

They walked together out into the hall. 'What time do you want to pick me up tomorrow?'

'About eight?'

'That's fine. I'll scribble down my address and leave it on the hall table. You'd better hurry up to Lucy.'

'Thanks.' He smiled at her. He'd meant what he had said: she would be perfect. Everyone would think she was delightful, plus there was the added bonus that there were no complications. Afterwards they would both have a light-hearted laugh about their little pretence, then forget it.

Another growl of thunder and Lucy's cries intensified. 'I'd better go.' On impulse Mac reached to kiss Melissa on the cheek.

The scent of her skin was fresh, her hair soft and silky under his fingertips. The sensation of sensual sweetness caused a momentary flicker of a question to enter his clear reasoning. Then he dismissed it.

CHAPTER FOUR

MELISSA stood in front of the long mirror and studied her reflection with a studious attention to detail.

The long black dress fell almost to the floor. It was plain yet stylish, with tiny shoestring straps that crossed over low on her back.

Her hair was swept up away from her face, exposing the long creamy line of her neck. She wore no jewellery at all. The effect was surprisingly sophisticated.

She sprayed some perfume on her wrists and neck and told herself firmly that she had no need to be nervous. It didn't really matter what Mac Schofield thought about her appearance. This was just a bit of fun for heaven's sake!

The sound of the doorbell made her courage falter. That would be him. Her eyes slid to the small clock on her bedside table. He was exactly on time.

Melissa moved slowly through her apartment towards the front door, trying to compose herself. She wasn't attracted to Mac Schofield, she told herself over and over again, like some mantra that would ward off evil spirits.

She swung the door open, a confident smile firmly in place.

He was wearing a dark suit with a bright blue shirt and contrasting tie. He looked wonderful. She felt a warm flow of adrenalin as their eyes met.

'Hi.' It was all she could think of to say.

'Hi.' His eyes swept over her.

'I am ready; I'll just get my bag.' She stepped back to allow him to enter the hallway.

He followed her to the door of her lounge, watching her every movement.

'How's Lucy tonight?' she asked.

Mac found it hard to concentrate. He couldn't take his eyes off Melissa. He had known she was beautiful, but he hadn't really noticed just how sensational she was. 'She's fine…went down to sleep quite easily tonight.'

The dress moved silkily against her figure as she walked, emphasising her slender curves and the graceful elegance of her body. She picked up her evening bag and turned to look at him.

Aware that he had been staring, he tried to feign an interest in her apartment. 'Nice place you've got here.' His glance swept over the comfortable lounge. He liked her decor, a stylish mixture of country classics and modern design.

'I like it, but I chose it because of the garden.' She hesitated for a moment and then said to him, 'Have you time to have a look?'

'We've got plenty of time,' Mac said easily, walking farther in. 'Does your mother live here with you?'

Melissa shook her head. 'No. Mom lives with her sister in Florida. I wanted her to move back up here until her operation, but she wouldn't hear of it. She's fiercely independent.'

He followed her to the French doors at the far end of the room. He waited as she pulled back the curtains and flicked on a light switch. The courtyard outside was instantly bathed in twinkling soft lights placed cleverly amidst a riot of tropical colour.

It was only a small garden but each part of it was used to its advantage to create a perfectly private haven. In the centre a water feature bubbled from the mouth of an old-fashioned black iron pump, trickling down over wooden pails and splashing onto shiny pebbles in a soothing, cooling sound. Large white marguerite daisies nodded their heads around it and a swing chair was invitingly positioned to one side.

'I'm impressed,' Mac said honestly. 'Is it all your own design and work?'

'Yes. There was nothing out here when I first got the apartment. Now it's my retreat.' Melissa smiled. 'At the end of a long, hot day, I come home, have a shower, take a glass of wine and sit out here, away from the TV and the telephone.'

'And what do you think about?' he asked softly.

The question made her look up at him and smile. 'Sometimes I do a bit of sketching, plan the gardens that I'm working on. Sometimes I just sit and think how much I like my daisies.'

'Well, they've certainly got pride of place in your garden,' he grinned.

'Lovely, aren't they? A totally unpretentious, friendly flower.'

'I didn't realise that flowers had characters.'

'Didn't you?'

He stared at her for a moment. He didn't quite know how to take her. She was so open and vibrant, so quirky, and yet totally engaging. A bit like her unpretentious daisies.

'I thought everyone knew that.' She reached to switch off the lights. 'I suppose we had better go.'

He tried to turn his thoughts to the evening ahead. Before arriving here tonight, it was all he had been able to think of. Now he felt distracted. His eyes followed her around the lounge as she switched off some more lights. Through an open doorway he could see her bedroom. A large double bed was covered in a white and pink patchwork quilt.

He frowned to himself. Maybe he should have asked Tara to accompany him tonight. She would never have been such a distraction. She would have clung to his arm, chatted about her art gallery and had no more effect on him than if she was talking about paint drying. Yet along came this…gardener, who talked about plants and turned him on to such an extent that, for half an instant, he was tempted to forget his boss's party altogether.

'Have I told you that you look simply stunning tonight?' he said softly.

She turned at the door and smiled at him. 'Thank you.'

For a while neither of them spoke; it was as if they were unwilling to break the bizarre feeling of intimacy that had suddenly sprung up.

'I'm ready if you are?' Melissa said quietly.

'Yes…' He mentally shook himself. 'Yes, of course.'

John Bradford's house was bathed in lights. It was high on a hill, raised on stilts, and it was a very impressive place. Mac parked the car and then went round to open the door for Melissa, but she had already got out. She stood in the warm night air looking up at the house and at the array of very snazzy cars parked in front of it, and shivered. 'I hope you're not going to regret doing this, Mac,' she said suddenly.

'Why should I regret it? You're a definite asset,' he said firmly. 'J.B. will be bowled over when he meets you. The job is as good as in the bag.'

'Don't be overconfident. To be honest, I'm a bit nervous of saying something wrong and spoiling your chances.'

'There's no chance of that. Just be yourself.'

Melissa looked over at him askance. 'That's going to be a bit difficult, isn't it,' she said wryly, 'when I'm trying to pretend that I'm your wife?'

'Partner,' he corrected her. 'And I don't see why it should be difficult.' He took her hand as they walked up the steps to the front door. It was an instinctive gesture—the steps were steep, and she was wearing very high heels. 'Just do as we discussed and stick as closely to the truth as possible.'

'I don't think you've thought this thing through,' Melissa said suddenly. 'For instance, what happens when you are invited to the next party your boss throws, the next work function, and I'm not around?'

'Melissa, I've been with the company for over a year and this is the first invitation to the boss's house. By the time another one comes along I'll hopefully have the job I want and will be proving that I can do it very well, single parent or not.'

'So what will you do, then—tell them I've left you?'

'I'll cross that bridge when I come to it. Will you stop worrying?' He squeezed her hand as they stopped outside the front door.

'It's you that should be worried, not me,' Melissa murmured.

Mac looked down at her small hand held so firmly in his. He wasn't worried about this in the slightest, he thought. In fact it felt very right.

The door swung open, enveloping them in light and the babble of voices and music.

'Mac, come on in,' a delighted voice called to them from the far end of a large room packed full of people.

Melissa felt glad that Mac didn't let go of her. It felt good walking in hand in hand.

It was Mac's boss who had called to them. He was a large, heavy-set man of about fifty with thick grey hair and deep-set blue eyes. He had a cigar in one hand and a glass of whisky in the other but he put both down to shake Melissa's hand as Mac introduced them.

'So you are the guiding light behind Mac,' he said warmly. 'It's good to meet you.'

'I wouldn't go so far as to say I'm a guiding light.' Melissa couldn't help but laugh.

'Nonsense, I'm a great believer in that old adage "Behind every successful man there is a good woman".'

'And a surprised mother-in-law?' Melissa asked with a grin.

He laughed, and his eyes drifted over her with a look

of admiration. 'So what do you think about Mac being short-listed for this project in Vegas?' he asked, picking up his glass of whisky again.

The question caused a momentary stir of nerves, especially as Mac chose that moment to let go of her hand as someone claimed his attention.

'I think it's very exciting,' Melissa said, trying to sound as if she knew what she was talking about. 'He's a very talented architect. I know he's going to go far.'

'Yes…' J.B. nodded '…I think you are right.'

A waiter appeared at Melissa's elbow with a tray of champagne. She helped herself to a glass and glanced over at Mac.

He was deep in conversation with a very glamorous woman. She had long straight blonde hair and was almost as tall as Mac, and she was gazing into Mac's eyes as if he was the most fascinating man she had ever met.

'How long have you and Mac been married?' J.B. asked her, making her swing her attention firmly back on to him.

'We're not married, but we've been together about a year now.' Melissa felt a dart of annoyance that Mac had left her to field such questions, while he chatted up an attractive woman. The feeling had no sooner drifted into her mind than she felt Mac's arm steal around her waist.

'Is it really that long?' he asked, making her realise that he had been aware of their conversation all along. 'It feels more like a few days than a whole year.'

He grinned at her as she looked up into the darkness of his eyes.

'Mac is a bit of a smooth talker, isn't he?' the woman who was standing next to him put in wryly.

'He has his moments.'

The woman smiled. 'I'm Cheryl Galloway. I don't believe we have met before.'

'No, I don't believe we have,' Melissa said, introducing

herself and wondering if Mac had mentioned this woman to her during their dinner together.

'When Mac comes into the office we often invite him to join us for a drink after work,' Cheryl said. 'But he's always in a hurry to get home.'

'Now you know why,' Mac said with a grin, drawing Melissa closer to his side.

She was very aware of the sensual feeling the light touch of his hand stirred inside her. His closeness was somehow erotic, as was the feeling of his breath against her neck as he turned to speak to her.

'Cheryl is one of the architects short-listed for head of design in Vegas,' he said quietly against her ear.

Melissa could hardly concentrate on his words; he was having a very profound effect on her senses.

A few more people joined them and the conversation moved to the new project in Las Vegas. Mac introduced her, and she tried very hard to keep track of all the names.

'Enchanted,' one man said, taking her hand in his and raising it to his lips. Melissa didn't like the way he looked at her; there was a suggestive gleam in his eyes. As soon as he released her hand she stepped back from his vicinity with a polite smile and was momentarily parted from Mac.

A house plant on a table caught her attention. It was a beautiful cyclamen with vivid pink flowers, but the edges of its leaves were turning brown. She bent to have a closer look.

'My daughter bought me that for Mother's Day last year,' a voice said beside her. 'I've been nursing it, but it's still not looking well.'

'I think it's in the wrong position here,' Melissa said, glancing over at the woman. She was in her mid-fifties with attractive silver-white hair and a trim figure. 'And you could be allowing it to dry out. These plants don't like to be too hot and they need reasonably well-drained moist soil.'

'Really?' The woman listened with interest. 'Are you one of the designers who is going to be working on the gardens at the new casino?'

'No. I'm…Melissa Barnes, Mac's partner,' Melissa said hesitantly.

'Mac?' The older woman's eyes moved over the gathering. 'Now, is he the tall, good-looking guy?'

'That's him,' Melissa said with a smile.

'Yes, I met him at the office once. Not that I go there all that often. J.B. spends enough time there for both of us. I'm Nancy, by the way—J.B.'s wife.'

Mac was desperately trying to concentrate on what Cheryl was saying, but his attention kept wandering over to Melissa. Somehow they had managed to get separated and he could no longer hear what she was talking about. She was deep in conversation with J.B.'s wife. Nancy seemed to be enthralled with whatever Melissa was saying. J.B. had wandered over and was talking to her as well. Mac could hear his laughter booming out over everything else.

'Your wife seems to be amusing J.B. greatly,' Cheryl said, suddenly changing the subject.

'Yes.'

'How long have you two been married?'

'We've been together for a year.'

'So you met after coming to work for the company?'

'That's right.' Mac wanted to get away. He glanced over as there was another wild guffaw of laughter from J.B.

'You have a little girl, don't you?'

'Yes, Lucy. She's mine by my first marriage.' Mac looked back to Cheryl. 'Excuse me, will you, Cheryl?' he said briskly and, before she could detain him for a moment longer, he moved through the crowds until he reached Melissa's side.

'You never told us that Melissa is a garden designer…'

J.B. rounded on Mac immediately '…and that she knows Simon.'

Mac was a little taken aback by the jovial accusation. The most personal his conversation with J.B. had ever got was when he had asked last week how the family was. 'Simon?' he said now, not able to place the name for a moment.

'Simon Wesley. My old boss…darling,' Melissa reminded him with a smile.

'Oh, yes.' For a moment he wondered if there was an edge to her voice, a sudden nervousness in the softness of her eyes. What had she told him about Simon Wesley? He racked his brains. Nothing untoward as he recalled, just how she had worked with him and how talented he was.

'Come and have a look at the plants in my conservatory, Melissa. Maybe you can give me some tips about them,' Nancy said, taking hold of her arm and leading her away before Mac could say anything further.

'What a delightful young woman,' J.B. remarked as he watched her walk away from them.

'Yes, isn't she?' Mac spoke almost to himself.

'You didn't tell me that her mother was from Texas like me, from the very same neighbourhood.'

'Didn't I?' Mac glanced after Melissa. He didn't know what spell she had cast over J.B., but Mac had never heard him this open and relaxed. Usually he just talked business.

'She reminds me of my youngest daughter.' He took a sip of his drink and eyed Mac thoughtfully over the glass.

'Nancy and I are going out to Vegas at the end of the week. Why don't you and Melissa come and join us at the ranch for the weekend?'

Mac wondered if he looked as stunned by the sudden invitation as he felt. J.B. wasn't known for being on friendly terms with his staff; he was a tough businessman. If he invited you for the evening to his house, you thought you'd really struck gold…but to be asked for a weekend to his ranch was unheard of. He was very tempted to just accept. But then he thought about Melissa. He'd never get her to agree to a second round of this charade. 'I'm sorry, J.B., but we have a young baby and no babysitter for the weekend—'

'Yes, Melissa was telling me all about Lucy and what a devoted father you are. You must bring the baby with you,' J.B. said firmly. 'And then we can talk some more about this project in Vegas.' He slapped Mac on the back, in a hearty, man-to-man kind of gesture. 'You're going to go far in this company, Mac…I like your style.'

Then he was striding away to talk to someone else, leaving Mac feeling slightly dazed.

What had brought that on? he wondered. Whatever it was, it sounded as if he stood a good chance of getting this job in Vegas.

Across the room he saw Melissa returning from the conservatory. She was laughing with Nancy about something, an animated sparkle in her eyes.

As he watched, a man went over towards her and tapped her on the shoulder. She turned and looked up at him. Even from this distance he could see the sudden pallor of her skin, the uncertainty in her eyes.

Who the heck was that? Mac wondered with a sinking feeling as he watched the man kissing her on the cheek. Obviously someone she knew. He hoped it wasn't someone who could blow the gaff on their little charade.

Apprehensively he moved across towards them.

'I'm glad I came to this party now,' he was saying. 'It's made my evening seeing you.'

Mac frowned, not liking the sound of this, or the way Melissa was looking up at him.

Mac put him at about forty-five. Not a bad-looking guy, with dark hair that was greying around the temples, and blue eyes that seemed glued to Melissa's face. He hardly looked away from her as Mac joined them.

'There you are, darling. I was wondering where you had got to.' Mac put an arm around her waist, then impulsively kissed the side of her face.

'Oh, hi.' Her voice was momentarily breathless, her skin slightly pink.

His kiss had flustered her, Mac noticed, wondering if it was because of the man standing next to her. Was she interested in him?

'This is my old boss, Simon Wesley. You remember— J.B. and I were just talking about him.'

'I do indeed.' Mac relaxed a little. At least it wasn't someone she had recently dated. He shook the other man by the hand. 'Pleased to meet you. I'm Mac Schofield.'

'So, what are you doing here, Simon?' Melissa asked once the formalities were observed.

'I know J.B. pretty well. I've done some freelance work for the company over the years. What about you?'

Melissa hesitated. 'I'm here with Mac. He's an architect with the firm.'

'Are you going to be working on this new project in Las Vegas?' Simon asked Mac conversationally.

'I hope to be.'

Simon nodded. 'They've called me in as design consultant for the gardens. It should prove quite a challenge.' His attention returned to Melissa. Mac noticed the way he glanced at her left hand as if checking for rings. 'Have you still got the garden centre?'

'No. I sold it a while ago. I work there for Kurt now.'

Loud music interrupted the conversation as a small orchestra struck up, and a few couples started to dance.

'Shall we dance, Melissa?' Mac asked smoothly. And without waiting for her reply he steered her away from Simon Wesley with a polite smile.

'Are you OK?' he asked, taking her into his arms.

'Yes, of course.' She tried to ignore the tight feeling in her chest. Of all the people to bump into, why did it have

to be Simon? She felt slightly sick inside. She hadn't seen
her ex-fiancé since they had called the wedding off.

'It's just that you seemed to be a bit…I don't know,
distracted or something.' Mac held her closer to him.

'Did I?' She closed her eyes. She didn't want to talk
about Simon—she couldn't go into that particular cauldron
of emotion right now.

'Yes.' He hesitated. 'It's a bit of bad luck running into
your ex-boss.'

Her body was pressed against his as more people joined
the dancing on the small parquet floor. She leaned her head
against his chest. 'I don't think it matters,' she murmured
quietly, and, surprisingly, she suddenly felt that she meant
it. It didn't matter. She was over Simon. It was just the
shock of seeing him. When J.B. had mentioned that he
was working on the casino her first thought had been, Dear
God, don't let him be here! And then, when she'd seen
him, the distress had been intense. She had wished that she
were anywhere in the world other than here. But now, in
Mac's arms, suddenly it didn't matter. 'It's ages since I
saw him, over a year ago. I don't think he presents any
threat to…what we've told J.B.'

Over her shoulder Mac could see Simon watching them.
He wasn't so sure that she was right. OK, Simon couldn't
contradict what they had told J.B. But there was something
about the way the guy looked at Melissa that rang alarm
bells inside him. He was a little too interested in her.

More people converged on the dance floor, and Mac
steered her protectively so she didn't get jostled, his hand
resting on the bare skin of her back where the dress dipped
low. It was an unintentional move, but it felt good. Her
skin was satiny soft under his fingertips and he found himself brushing them lightly over her.

It was an infinitesimal, whisper-soft caress, yet the effect
was explosive through Melissa's body. It caused a delicious, shivery sensation inside her, and made tingles of

awareness race down her spine. She wondered if he realised what he was doing to her—perhaps it was an act for
any onlookers?

Mac liked the scent of her perfume, liked being this
close. She had a very sensuous body; it swayed against
him very provocatively, creating a ripple of desire inside
him. If he lowered his head fractionally, his lips would be
close to hers.

The idea made him pull back. He had asked Melissa
here tonight for business reasons, he reminded himself
sharply.

'Shall we go and get another drink?' he said suddenly,
letting go of her.

'If you want.' She looked up at him, her eyes searching
his.

'Yes.' He turned away. 'It's very hot in here, don't you
think?'

They stood by some open patio doors. Melissa helped
herself to another glass of champagne, Mac chose a glass
of Coke. Across the room Melissa could see Simon. Her
eyes followed him coolly as he talked to various people.
It was hard to believe that this was the man who had hurt
her so badly. Now that she had recovered from the shock
of seeing him again, she felt nothing—no regrets, no heart-
wrenching anxiety, nothing.

'J.B. certainly likes you.' Mac interrupted her thoughts.
'He said that you reminded him of his youngest daughter.'

'Did he?' Melissa was quiet for a moment. 'His youngest daughter died in a car accident ten years ago.'

'How do you know that?' Mac asked, dismayed.

'Nancy told me when we were alone in the conservatory. It's still a source of great sadness for them both. After
her death J.B. immersed himself in his business and
achieved its great success.'

Mac watched her, noting the soft compassion in her
eyes, the gentleness about her. 'People open up to you,

don't they, Melissa?' he remarked suddenly. 'We've been here...' he glanced at his watch '...a couple of hours, and already you know more about my employer than I've found out in a year.'

'Well, I'm a woman. We tend to talk more on a personal level, get to the heart of things,' she said with a teasing gleam in her eyes. 'I suppose all you and J.B. talk about is work and maybe baseball if you're feeling particularly reckless.'

'If I'd have said that you would have branded me a chauvinist,' Mac remarked wryly.

She grinned. 'I'd have been right.'

He shook his head and smiled. 'You're wrong about one thing. We never talk about baseball at work. We never get that reckless.'

'I suppose it's pretty pressurised at the office.'

'There isn't much time for social pleasantries,' he agreed. 'But then again, maybe it's just as well, because if there was everyone would know all my business and you wouldn't be here with me now.' He reached out and touched the side of her face. It was just a gentle caress, but it made Melissa feel as if her skin was on fire.

She looked up at him from beneath long, dark lashes. 'You're not flirting with me, are you, Mac?'

The direct question seemed to take him aback. 'Would you mind if I was?'

She laughed and sipped her champagne. 'I suppose a little harmless flirting never hurt anyone.'

'And we have to keep up appearances,' he agreed. 'For instance your ex-boss appears to be watching us very closely.'

'Does he?' Suddenly the champagne tasted flat, the bubbles evaporating along with the lightness of her mood. Mac was keeping up a façade, playing to the gallery; he wasn't flirting with her at all.

It was incomprehensible how that knowledge could

make her feel slightly depressed. She didn't know Mac Schofield. She was playing a part; she had no right to feel like this.

She glanced over at Simon. Mac was right—he was looking over at her. She glanced quickly away. 'Maybe he still finds me attractive,' she said impulsively. 'He used to tell me quite frequently that he thought I was gorgeous.' So eat your heart out, Mac Schofield, she thought fiercely. Some men would like to flirt with me for real.

She glanced up at Mac. He didn't look impressed and she immediately felt foolish. Why on earth did you say that? she asked herself wildly. And about Simon Wesley of all people! 'But that was a long time ago,' she muttered, trying to backtrack.

'I thought you said he was your boss?'

'He was.' She took a deep breath and decided to lighten everything up again, make a joke, let him know that she hadn't for one moment imagined that he might really be flirting with her. 'Anyway, back to our little subterfuge. It's quite amusing, isn't it, playing at being partners? A bit like being a kid again and playing at mummies and daddies!'

He laughed at that. 'Not quite, Melissa, but I get your drift.'

He finished his drink and put the empty glass down. 'Would you like another glass of champagne?'

She looked down, surprised to see that she was nursing an empty glass. 'Why not?' Melissa smiled at him.

She watched as he walked across the room to fetch her one, noticing how the women looked at him. He was certainly handsome...a real head-turner. She shouldn't be too hard on herself. It was easy to fall under the spell of a man like that and read too much into the way he smiled at you, the way he brushed against you. Those good looks and that dangerous air of sensuality were a lethal combination. Men like Mac veered towards being smooth oper-

ators. One minute they were smiling into your eyes, the
next, breaking your heart. She'd have to be wary.

Speaking of which, she noticed that Simon was making
his way over towards her. Hell! She tried to pretend she
hadn't noticed, turning her back to him a little, hoping he'd
get the hint.

'Hi. Not talking to me?' He scooted around her and
looked teasingly into her eyes.

'I talked to you a little while ago.' She smiled at him
politely. 'I thought we'd said all there was to say?'

'You know that's not true.' His voice was gentle, coax-
ing. 'I didn't tell you how never a day goes by without
me regretting what happened between us.'

'Oh, come on, Simon!' she hissed. 'I don't want to hear
that now. Besides,' she added, 'I'm with Mac and I'm very
happy. What happened between us is history.'

He nodded. 'It's serious, then, this affair with
Schofield?'

'Yes. Very,' she said quickly, then found herself wishing that she were speaking the truth. Heavens, what was
the matter with her? she wondered. Maybe she shouldn't
have another glass of champagne.

Mac had been waylaid by Nancy. He tried to concentrate
on what she was saying to him but his eyes kept veering
over towards Melissa. He watched with a feeling of irri-
tation as Simon leaned closer towards her, and put one
finger under her chin to tip her face up towards his.

'So, J.B. has invited you and Melissa to the ranch,'
Nancy was saying to him. 'I do hope you will both come.
J.B., of course, will be caught up with this casino business,
but Melissa and I could do a little shopping.'

'Thank you for the invitation, Nancy,' he said quietly.
'I'm just not sure how free we are next weekend. I'll have
to check with Melissa.'

He couldn't expect Melissa to go away with him for the

weekend, he told himself sternly. However tempting the notion.

He glanced back over at her and frowned as he saw Simon reach into the inside pocket of his jacket and bring out a card to give her. Was he chatting her up? Indignation washed over Mac. The guy had a damned nerve.

Melissa smiled brightly at Mac as he returned.

'Your admirer has abandoned you, I see,' he said wryly as he handed her the glass of champagne.

'Who? Oh, Simon—yes.'

He noticed how her skin flushed pink. Was she attracted to Simon Wesley?

'You know, I think we should really be making tracks, after you've finished your drink,' he said, glancing at his watch. 'I did tell Patricia we wouldn't be late home.'

'Yes, all right.' She tried to keep the disappointment from her voice. She didn't want to leave; she had hoped that Mac would ask her to dance again.

Mac noticed the dismay in her eyes and felt a tug of severe annoyance. Obviously Simon Wesley held a great attraction.

She took a couple of sips of her drink and then put it down. 'Well, as you are obviously in a hurry, I'd better say goodbye to Nancy.'

They went to find their hosts.

'You're not leaving already?' Nancy sounded disappointed.

'Sorry, but we've got to,' Mac said firmly. 'We've got a babysitter waiting.'

'Well, never mind. Hopefully we'll see you and Melissa next weekend.'

'What did Nancy mean about next weekend?' Melissa asked as they walked away.

'I'll tell you later,' Mac murmured, wondering what the hell he was going to do about that invitation.

He turned and led the way outside into the night air. It

was pleasantly warm. The stars were bright in the Milky Way, and the sound of the surf pounding against the shore behind the house filled the air.

'Did J.B. say anything about the job you want?' Melissa linked her arm through his as they went down the steps.

'In a roundabout way. It sounded promising.'

'So I fit the criteria of perfect partner, then?'

'I think you were a hit.' He glanced down at her. The moonlight was playing softly over her features. Her skin looked very pale against the darkness of her surroundings. His eyes moved to where her dress dipped into the hollow of her breast. 'Possibly too much of a hit.'

She frowned. 'What do you mean by that?'

'Nothing.' He shook his head. 'Pay no attention to me.'

What the heck was the matter with him? he wondered grimly as he unlocked the car door for her to get in and then went round to the driver's side.

Melissa had been wonderful tonight. Everyone had been totally smitten with her. So why did he feel so on edge? She had done all that he'd asked of her and more. J.B. was eating out of his hand: he had even invited them to his ranch in Nevada for the weekend. Was that what was troubling him? The fact that he'd have to turn down that invitation?

He started the car and pulled down the drive and out onto the highway.

'What do you mean, too much of a hit?' Melissa frowned, unable to leave the subject.

'If you must know, I wasn't too happy about Simon Wesley giving you his phone number in full view of the whole room,' Mac said abruptly, then wished he hadn't. He sounded jealous.

Melissa turned to look at him. 'Why?'

Mac shrugged. 'I just think you could have been a bit more discreet.'

'I beg your pardon?' She frowned.

'You were flirting with him, Melissa. And everyone could see you.'

'I wasn't flirting with him.' She was taken aback.

'It looked very cosy to me.'

There was a deep silence for a moment. He pulled the car into her road and to a standstill in front of her apartment. 'I'm sorry,' he said heavily. 'I know I've no right to say this to you, but I would have appreciated it if you could have been a bit more discreet, considering our circumstances.'

'I don't know what the hell you are talking about.' Melissa was furious now. 'If you must know, I was trying to get away from Simon, but he insisted on apologising profusely to me for something that happened in the past. Then he went on to talk about work. He was giving me his phone number because he's looking for a new assistant and he thinks I'd be perfect for the job.' She glared at him. 'You're not the only one preoccupied with your career, Mac Schofield.' She grasped the door-handle, anxious to get away.

He caught up with her as she reached her front door. 'Melissa.'

'What?' She didn't look round.

'I overreacted and I'm sorry.'

'It doesn't matter.' Melissa slipped her front-door key in the lock.

'It does matter because I've upset you.'

'No, you haven't,' she lied.

'I'm not usually so on edge. I don't know what got into me.'

She released her breath in a sigh and turned to look at him.

'Am I forgiven?' He looked at her with a raised eyebrow.

It was hard not to forgive him when he looked at her

like that. She found herself softening. 'Yes. You're forgiven.'

'So we're friends again? Hmm?' He moved closer to
her.

'Yes, we're friends.' She looked up into the darkness of
his eyes, at the firm, attractive line of his lips. She remembered how good it had felt to be held by him as they'd
danced.

'Are you going to invite me in for a coffee?'

She hesitated. 'Didn't you tell Patricia you wouldn't be
late?'

'It's only eleven.' He smiled ruefully. 'Besides, that was
a little white lie. Patricia is staying over tonight; she said
it didn't matter what time I was home.'

CHAPTER FIVE

'YOU have two messages on your answering machine,' Mac remarked as she made the coffee.

'Press "play",' Melissa instructed.

He did so, and a woman's voice filled the room. 'Sorry I missed you earlier, Mel. I'm fine; please don't worry about me.'

'My mother,' Melissa informed him, coming back into the room with the tray of coffee. 'And she's a master when it comes to playing things down; she's anything but fine.'

The message ended and another one started. A man's voice this time. 'You left without saying goodbye,' it accused. 'It was great seeing you again, Melissa, and I meant what I said to you. Ring me.'

Mac recognised Simon Wesley's voice immediately. 'He's a fast worker. How did he get your number?'

'He must have it from last year,' Melissa replied nonchalantly.

'Does he have this address as well?'

'No. I've moved since Simon had my address.'

Mac watched as Melissa poured the coffee. He noticed that her hand wasn't quite steady.

'So, what was he apologising to you for?'

'What?' Coffee splashed into one of the saucers. 'Sorry, I'll just go and fix this.' She picked up the cup and saucer and headed towards the kitchen.

'You told me he was apologising for something in the past,' Mac continued, undeterred, as soon as she returned. He wanted to know Melissa's feelings for the guy.

'I think it had something to do with the fact that while

he was engaged to me he was sleeping with my best friend.' She kept her voice deliberately light.

'Simon Wesley was your fiancé?' Mac looked astonished. Then he cringed. 'Oh, hell, Melissa, I'm sorry. I'd no idea.'

'Why should you? It's OK.'

He raked a hand through his hair. 'It must have been a very awkward evening for you…'

'Well, I must admit it was a shock seeing him after all this time.'

'You haven't seen him since the break-up?'

She shook her head. 'But it was cool; we were OK. I think he was genuinely sorry for what he put me through, and he was glad of the opportunity to tell me.'

'Is he still with your friend, the girl he betrayed you with?'

'No.' She sighed. 'He said at the time that it had been a mistake, that it had only happened once. That he still loved me.' For a moment her voice faltered. 'But I couldn't believe him.'

'So now he wants to take up where you left off?'

'No. Nothing like that. I told you, he just offered me a job. I don't know if it was his way of trying to make amends or if he just honestly thought that I would be right for the position.'

'I can guess what position he had in mind,' Mac said dryly.

'Mac!'

'Sorry.' He looked over at her. 'How did you feel, seeing him again?'

'I told you, it was a shock. Look, do you mind if we don't talk about this? I'd rather just forget about it.'

'Sure.' Mac nodded. But he wanted to know more; he wanted to get inside her head and find out what she was thinking, feeling. He fought the temptation. After all, it was none of his business. 'I don't want to ask insensitive questions,' he murmured. 'I know what it feels like when a love affair goes wrong.'

'Yes, I suppose you do.'

He looked over at her and the warmth and understanding in her eyes were profoundly unsettling. He glanced away. 'So, do you think you might take up this job offer from Wesley?'

'I don't think so. Anyway, you don't need to worry about him, Mac,' she said with a shake of her head. 'Yes, he knows your boss, but I hardly think they will be comparing telephone numbers to see if yours matches mine. I think our secret's safe.'

She leaned over to pour more coffee. He could see the edge of her bra which was a pretty black lace one. She had a very desirable body. It curved in all the right places. 'I wasn't thinking about the consequences of our charade.' He spoke impulsively, following his instincts.

She looked over at him, a flicker of heat stirring inside her at the sudden note of serious intent in his voice. 'What were you thinking about?'

Mac hesitated. 'Well, I was hoping you were going to stick around for a while,' he said truthfully.

'Were you?' Melissa felt confusion and desire racing around at one and the same time. The sensation was deeply disturbing. 'Why?'

Mac hesitated. 'Well, for one, I don't want to lose you out of my garden; you're doing too good a job.' There was a teasing glint in his eye.

She smiled, a trifle unsteadily. 'Thanks. But Kurt has quite a few good designers on his team. I could be replaced very easily.'

'I don't think so.'

Again there was that disturbing undertone of sensuality in his voice. She wondered if she was imagining it. But, real or imagined, Melissa felt her body responding to him in the most sharply disconcerting way. It was like a fierce thrust of adrenalin, unlike anything she had ever known. What would it be like to kiss him, she wondered, to be crushed close against that powerful, fantastic body?

She put her coffee cup down. She would have to be very careful. Mac had a dangerous combination of charm and sex appeal. But this wasn't a date as such, and she didn't want him to think she was an easy bet.

Mac saw the shadows of uncertainty in her eyes. He tore his eyes away from her, trying to think about something else, anything that would cool the ferocious heat of an ardour that had risen so rapidly, so unexpectedly. Melissa was doing him a favour, pretending to be his partner. He couldn't let a moment of desire complicate that.

There was a black and white photograph on the mantelpiece; he trained his attention on it instead. 'Who's in the photo?'

'Mum and Dad. It was taken on their wedding day.' Had she just imagined the way he had looked at her, the need in his eyes? Melissa had never found it so hard to read signals before. Usually she knew when a man wanted her…and she could have sworn…

'Where is your dad now?'

'He died when I was ten.' Her voice held a husky note for just a second.

'That must have been hard.'

'Yes, it was. I still miss him. Mum found it very difficult bringing me up on her own. Money was very tight. That's why she sold the family home and moved us to live with her sister in Florida.'

'The family home being in Texas?'

'That's right.' She looked over at him in surprise.

'J.B. mentioned your mother was from Texas.' He smiled. 'You see, we did talk about something other than work tonight.'

'Very daring.' She grinned.

'It must be the effect you have on me.'

There was a moment of silence, a moment when Melissa's heart seemed to miss a beat and then move on. Their eyes locked. She really liked Mac Schofield. Liked his warmth, his humour as much as his good looks. Then he smiled, and the warmth cooled, as if shutters were being pulled down over the dark velvet of his eyes.

'Can I ask you a personal question now?' she said impulsively.

'Depends what it is.' He tried to make a joke. But that direct, steady gaze of hers never failed to disconcert him.

'You said earlier that you knew what it felt like to be hurt.'

'Did I?'

She heard the wariness in his tone now.

'I just wondered if perhaps you deliberately hide behind work because it's safe.'

'How do you mean?'

'Well, I know when my engagement to Simon fell through I did push all my energy into business. It was somehow easier to occupy all my thoughts and all my strength at work because it saved me having to dwell on personal, painful facts. Maybe you are doing the same? Locking yourself away?'

'I don't think so, Melissa.' His voice was carefully cool. Yet through that controlled, icy demeanour Melissa sensed that she had hit a nerve.

'Sorry.' She winced. 'I shouldn't have said that, should I? It's one of my failings. I tend to jump in impulsively and say what's running through my mind.'

It was hard to remain defensive in the face of such a sincere apology. Mac smiled. 'I don't think that's a failing. Not in you anyway.'

'So, if I was to ask you why your wife left, you wouldn't think I was being too nosy?'

'No.' He was silent for a moment. 'She left because she wanted her career more than she wanted a baby.' There was no bitterness in the statement; it was just flat and matter-of-fact. Then he shrugged. 'Lucy wasn't planned, you see. Kay found herself pregnant and wasn't happy. I was ecstatic. You can imagine the arguments.'

'Couldn't she have had both—the career and the child? A lot of women do.'

'That wasn't how Kay wanted her life to run. She thought that view was very naive, that no woman could have it all.' His voice was bleak for a moment. 'I tried to persuade her that she could. It wasn't really fair of me, I suppose. And maybe I was idealistic. I thought that once she held Lucy she would change her mind. But she didn't.'

'I'm sorry, Mac. It must have been a difficult time for both you and Kay.'

He looked across at the sympathy in her face, at the wide violet-blue eyes. 'Yes, it was.'

The reply was simple, no real emotion in the tone of his voice, or the darkness of his eyes. Yet Melissa intuitively sensed that behind that steely façade lay an abundance of feeling. She wanted to say, You're not over Kay, are you? The words wavered precariously on the edge of being spoken, then she thought better of it. She was theorising. Maybe he was over his ex-wife. And, whether he was or not, it wasn't her place to speculate.

He glanced at his watch. 'You know, I suppose I should be going. Even though Patricia is staying, I don't like to be away from Lucy for long at night.'

She watched as he finished his drink, and wished he would stay a little longer. He stood up and she followed him towards the front door.

'How about having lunch with me tomorrow?' he offered suddenly. 'My way of saying thank you for tonight.' He turned and looked down into her eyes.

She was sorely tempted to accept but, for reasons that had nothing to do with accepting his gratitude, Melissa shook her head regretfully. 'There's no need to thank me. I enjoyed this evening.'

She was aware that her refusal surprised him.

He frowned and then, just as he had done at the party, he reached out to touch her face. 'Can't I persuade you?' he murmured.

She felt the slow thud of her heart against her chest. Mac Schofield sent out too many conflicting signals. One moment he was implying that this was strictly platonic, the next he was looking at her as if he was truly falling for her. The touch of his hand against her skin was light but it stirred up a flurry of emotional reactions, not one of which could pass for anything light-hearted or platonic.

'I know a restaurant that does a great Sunday lunch. Lucy and I would really welcome your company.'

It was the mention of Lucy that swung it, or so she tried to tell herself. She nodded in agreement before she had even formulated the words of acceptance.

'Great. I'll pick you up at one.' He bent down towards her. His lips brushed softly against hers, then he pulled back and looked down into her eyes.

The touch of his lips, the closeness of his body sent her senses into chaos. She struggled to get a breath, to think coherently.

'See you tomorrow, then,' he said.

'Yes. Tomorrow.' She could hardly get the words to formulate in her mind.

He leaned down and kissed her again. This time there was no hesitation; it was a hard, demanding kiss filled with a sensuality that seemed to explode somewhere deep inside Melissa.

He didn't touch her at all, but she wanted him to. She leaned closer against him, feeling the heaviness of her breast against his chest. Her hands rested on the soft material of his jacket.

He stepped back. 'Well, goodnight, then.'

CHAPTER SIX

THE waves made a thundering hiss against the sandy shore as they rolled in from the Pacific. A few seagulls wheeled overhead, crying out in a mocking way as if they knew secrets withheld from the humans who walked along the pier below.

Lucy wanted to be out of her pram. She protested against its constraints loudly, wriggling and kicking her legs until Mac gave up and lifted her out.

Now she toddled unsteadily between them, in her pink check romper suit, stamping her feet on the wooden boards of the pier, with a look of utter enjoyment on her face.

'And that's why my dates don't usually want Lucy around,' Mac pointed out.

Melissa found it hard to believe that any woman could fail to think Lucy was adorable. 'She's a very determined young lady,' Melissa said. 'And I'm quite sure all your dates fall in love with her.'

Lucy looked up at her with a smile as if she approved of that statement, her big blue eyes wide with merriment.

Melissa felt her heart melt.

Mac laughed. 'I don't think so. In fact the last time I took Tara out she asked me if I was considering which school to send her to and suggested a couple of real good ones—both took boarders.'

'Oh, come on! She had to be joking. She's only a baby, for heaven's sake!'

'That's what I thought. But she was very serious. Said you had to think ahead.'

Melissa's eyebrows rose. 'She doesn't sound like a very nice person, Mac.'

'Maybe you're right.' He laughed suddenly. 'But perhaps you'd think differently if you'd been kept awake all night by Lucy. I don't mind because she's my daughter and I love her to bits, but for anyone else it's just an inconvenience.'

A picture rose in Melissa's mind. A picture of Tara staying over at Mac's house, making love with him. Then the interruption of Lucy's cries. She didn't like the picture; she desperately tried to blank it out.

She glanced over at Mac. He was wearing jeans and an open-necked blue shirt. He looked relaxed and happy as he watched his daughter. He also looked incredibly handsome. She noticed, as the summer breeze ruffled his dark hair, that there were a few grey hairs at his temples.

Melissa also noticed the way his hand hovered protectively next to Lucy in case she should fall. Something tightened in her chest. She could really fall for Mac Schofield in a big way.

He looked over at her and smiled. 'Hope you're hungry. They do great food out here.'

'So I've heard. I've never eaten here before, but perhaps that's because I'm not one of the trendy crowd.'

'Really?' His eyes moved over her slender figure in the stylish white sundress. 'You look like one.'

'Thanks.' She laughed. 'I think.'

As they reached the door to the restaurant Mac folded the pram, and Melissa took hold of Lucy's hand to lead her inside.

The decor was extremely pleasing—polished wooden floors and balustrades which gave the impression of being on the deck of a ship. Even though it was busy, they got a seat in the far window with views out across the ocean.

A high chair was brought for Lucy and placed at the end of the table between them. They ordered their drinks and Mac reached into the pram and took out a bottle of juice for Lucy.

'You're very organised,' Melissa remarked.

'I've got to be,' he said with a grin. 'There is no such thing as travelling light when you've got a baby.'

The waitress arrived and handed them their drinks and menus. She smiled at Lucy. 'You're so cute,' she said, bending down to talk to her. 'Yes, you are,' she cooed. 'A real little beauty.' She glanced over at Melissa. 'How old is she?'

It was obvious that the woman thought she was the child's mother. 'Fourteen months,' Melissa answered, wondering if she should make it clear that she wasn't.

'About the same age as my little boy.' The woman smiled. 'Quite a handful at this stage, aren't they?'

'Well, I—'

'I bet you keep Mummy and Daddy busy.'

As the woman hastened away again, Melissa wondered if she looked as flustered as she felt. She glanced across at Mac.

He was watching her with an absorbed interest which made her feel even more awkward for some reason.

'Sorry about that; I did try to tell her she'd got it wrong.'

He shrugged. 'It was a natural mistake for her to make. No big deal. Probably better just to go with it, otherwise she'd feel embarrassed for getting it wrong.'

'I suppose so.' Melissa took a sip of her cocktail. She met Mac's eyes across the table and found herself remembering the way he had kissed her last night.

What was he thinking about? she wondered. Had that kiss meant anything?

'The party went all right last night, didn't it?' she said, trying to fill the sudden silence between them.

He smiled. 'Yes. It seemed to.'

'When do you think you'll find out about your job?'

'I don't know. But, as patience isn't one of my virtues, I hope it's going to be soon.'

'J.B. didn't strike me as the indecisive type so I suppose it won't take him long to make up his mind.'

Mac had a sudden vivid memory of J.B.'s smiling face and the invitation to the casino site. Melissa was probably right. But if he didn't take J.B. up on that invitation, would the job go decisively to someone else?

'We should really ring Nancy and thank her for her hospitality,' Melissa continued blithely, unaware that Mac's thoughts had wandered. 'If you give me her number, I'll do it. That's if you want me to, of course?'

The waitress interrupted them to take their orders. As neither of them had got round to even glancing at the menus, they hurriedly turned their attention towards them.

'Where were we?' Melissa asked, once they were left alone again.

'You were offering to ring Nancy.'

'Oh, yes. I just thought, as I'm supposed to be your partner, she might expect me to ring. Also, she was asking me last night about one of her plants in the conservatory and I was thinking about it afterwards, wondering if perhaps it should be outside, not under glass at all. I wanted to have another word with her about it. Really, I should have asked Simon for his opinion, but my brain wasn't properly in gear at the party.'

'I should think you know just as much about plants as Simon Wesley does,' Mac said firmly.

'Thanks for the vote of confidence, but it's a very rare type of orchid. Simon is a whizz at knowing things like that. He's quite brilliant actually.'

'Really.' For some reason Mac couldn't quite eliminate the dry note in his voice.

'Oh, yes. In fact, maybe I'll give him a ring and ask him about it. If he goes round and looks at the plant, he's bound to know it. He's got an almost photographic memory.'

'He forgot he was engaged to you, though, didn't he?'

As soon as he saw the dark shadows clouding the beauty of her eyes, Mac regretted the wisecrack. 'Sorry,' he murmured. 'I guess I don't much like the guy.'

'Why?'

Mac shrugged. 'Maybe because I know he hurt you, and I happen to like you.'

The warmth of Mac's voice distracted her. Made her wish that he would go a bit further than just liking her. She tore her eyes away from his, disturbed by the sensual power he could wield over her senses with just a few casual words.

'Simon's OK.' Melissa toyed with the napkin on her plate. In truth her mind was far away from her ex-fiancé. She wished she could get a handle on Mac Schofield, work out if he was interested in her romantically.

'You've decided to forgive him, then?'

'No point in holding on to grudges; life's too short.'

'I suppose you're right,' Mac agreed. 'But you should also learn by your mistakes. If he's hurt you once, he could do it again.'

'I don't intend to give him the opportunity.'

Something about the way she refused to look directly at him as they talked made him wonder how true that was. The idea that she might pick up where she had left off with Simon Wesley was most distasteful.

The waitress brought their meals and, for a while, Mac turned his attention to sorting out Lucy, putting her bib on and organising her lunch into the spare dish that the waitress had provided. But all the time he was thinking about Melissa phoning Simon Wesley. He wanted to stop her. Tell her it would be a great mistake. Trouble was, he knew he didn't have the right to make such sweeping remarks.

Lucy gurgled happily as he handed her a spoon to feed herself. Melissa smiled. 'Sounds like it won't be long before she's talking.'

'Yes, she's already saying a few words. Most of them indistinguishable.'

Melissa watched the child for a moment. With those wide blue eyes and golden curls, she looked as if she could have come straight out of a model agency. 'She's adorable, Mac. And so good-looking. You must be very proud of her.'

'I am.' Mac grinned over at her. 'But I can't really take much credit for the looks. I think she's a lot like her mother.'

'Has Kay got curly blonde hair?'

Mac shook his head. 'She's a blonde, but it's straight, not even a wave in it.'

Melissa conjured up a picture of a stunningly attractive, blue-eyed blonde with long straight hair.

'Do you see much of your ex-wife?'

'The last time I saw Kay she brought a present for Lucy on her first birthday. But she didn't stay long.'

'Doesn't she see Lucy on a regular basis?'

He shook his head.

Melissa looked over at the child in bewilderment. 'How can she bear not to see her?'

'I don't know,' Mac said quietly. 'It's a question I have asked myself many times. All I can say is that just because you are a woman it doesn't mean you have to be maternal...some women just aren't. Kay...isn't a bad person. As I told you last night, she just never wanted a baby.'

Melissa wanted to reach out to him, to soothe the sudden furrows in his brow.

'But there you go,' he continued briskly. 'One of life's little lessons. I've learnt from it and I've moved on.' He paused for a moment and then shrugged. 'Well, we've discussed your ex and mine. Shall we put the skeletons back in the closet and close the door on them?'

She smiled at that. 'Yes, good idea.'

She glanced over at Lucy who had now started to toy

with her food. Impulsively she reached to encourage the little girl to eat more. Spooning up the food, she held it to Lucy's lips. 'Come on, sweetheart, you can do better than that,' she murmured.

Mac watched her. Noticed the absorbed expression in the violet-blue of her eyes as she looked at his daughter. He couldn't remember any woman he had dated looking so much at home with her. He frowned.

'So, getting back to Nancy. Do you want me to phone her?' Melissa glanced across at him.

He shook his head. 'Maybe you'd better leave it to me.'

'Oh, OK.'

'Well, she'll only start asking you about her plants again, and then you'll feel obliged to ring Simon and it's getting a bit complex.'

'I don't mind.'

'Don't you?' He stared at her across the table. 'What part don't you mind? Ringing Simon, or playing at partners with me?'

'Well—'

'The thing is…' he interrupted her quietly '…that if it's the latter I could really use your help again.'

Melissa paused, the spoon wavering in mid-air as she looked at him.

'Last night at the party, Nancy and J.B. invited us to their ranch in Nevada for the weekend. I think if I go the job will be as good as mine. But they want us both to go, not just me.' He hadn't planned to say that; the words just kind of came out of their own volition.

'I've tried to turn the invitation down, of course,' he said hastily. 'I told them we had no babysitter. I thought that would get me off the hook, but J.B. told me to bring Lucy as well—he was most insistent. So was Nancy.'

Melissa was aware of a fierce stab of disappointment inside her. Her instincts had been correct. Mac was only interested in this damn pretence. She should never have allowed herself to hope that today was about anything else. He had made it pretty clear at the party last night that he hadn't been flirting with her, that it was strictly for the benefit of his boss. But, even so, in the privacy of her home he had kissed her goodnight.

That kiss had kept her awake for hours after he had gone. She had half convinced herself that perhaps there was a chance for a relationship to grow between them. That he wanted to get to know her better. Now it appeared that the only reason he had asked her out to lunch was to try and persuade her to go even deeper into the charade. Had he thrown in a passionate kiss last night for good measure?

'I'm sorry, Mac.' Her voice was stiff. 'My appearance as your make-believe steady partner was a once-only performance. I'm not doing it again.'

'Won't you even consider it?'

'The answer is no, Mac.' She glared at him. 'I suppose this is the reason you asked me out today?'

'No.' He frowned. 'I asked you out today because I wanted to spend some time in your company.'

Melissa would have liked to believe that, but she didn't think she could.

Mac watched her across the table and felt he had handled this badly. He really hadn't intended to ask her to masquerade as his partner again. It had been a wild whim. 'Honestly, Melissa. I really fully intended never mentioning J.B.'s invitation to you.'

'Well, I'm not doing it.' It was ridiculous to feel disappointment so acutely, but she couldn't help it. Lucy gave a little disgruntled cry and, realising that she was still waiting for her next mouthful of food, Melissa resumed feeding her. 'I mean it's just ridiculous. For a start, we wouldn't fool anybody that we were a real family. Lucy hardly knows me, for heaven's sake.'

'For someone who hardly knows Lucy, you're not doing

too badly with her,' Mac pointed out gently as she put the last spoonful of food in the baby's mouth. 'The waitress thought you were Lucy's mother.'

Melissa glared at him again. 'I'm not doing it, Mac,' she repeated.

'OK, no one is forcing you. I'm only asking.'

She finished feeding Lucy and then looked down at her plate of food. The meal was delicious, but she had suddenly lost her appetite.

'Maybe if you hadn't been quite so forthcoming at the party last night—like telling J.B. that your mother was from the same part of Texas as himself and being oh, so charming to Nancy, giving her helpful hints with her precious plants—we wouldn't have received the honoured invitation,' Mac grated suddenly.

'Oh, so now it's my fault?'

'No, but you were very friendly, Melissa. Come on, Nancy and you really were getting along like long-time buddies.'

The memory of Nancy, talking to her quietly in the conservatory about the loss of her youngest daughter, came into her mind. She had liked the woman a lot, had felt complete empathy with her. 'I was just being myself, Mac,' she said now, honestly.

'Well, maybe you should have held part of yourself back,' he suggested.

She wanted to say, Like you do? but she held the words. Maybe she had been a bit too open, had forgotten that it was a one-off meeting for her with J.B. and his wife. She had been interested in them, had liked them. '*You* told me to be myself,' she reminded him. 'You didn't tell me there were rules of deception…like don't get too familiar or involved.'

'I'm not blaming you for anything. You did wonderfully well. But look at it from my point of view now—I'm in an impossible situation. The fact that my employers want to see you again, the fact that they think you are the greatest thing since they invented baseball, is down to you. You can't blame me for asking for a repeat performance... I don't know what to do. I want the job and it seems that I now really do need you to clinch it.' His lips twisted ruefully. 'Maybe I am blaming you...it's your fault because you are too damn...captivating.'

'Don't try to whitewash me, Mac.' She frowned and wondered anew if that was what he had been doing when he had kissed her last night. Had he been flattering her, pretending an interest in her that he really didn't have? 'And I don't like baseball; as far as I'm concerned it wasn't such a great invention.'

'OK, maybe you're not as perfect as I first thought.' He spread his hands and fixed her with a teasing look.

She tried very hard not to let him make her smile. 'I did point out last night that this might happen. I asked you what you would do if we got another invitation as a couple. You told me not to worry, as I recall,' she finished dryly.

'How was I to know that everyone would fall in love with you?'

'Don't exaggerate,' she said crossly.

'I'm not.' His voice was earnest. 'For instance, I got to know my boss much better last night than I have in over a year, and it was all down to you.'

'Rubbish.'

'It's true. There's something about you. You're so radiant. You step into a room and you sparkle. You bring out the best side of a person's personality. With J.B., for instance. I've never seen him so affable.'

'That's in your imagination. He was probably more affable because he'd had a couple of drinks.'

'Well, his wife wasn't drinking. How do you explain that?'

Melissa shrugged. 'She's a lovely person; she'd get on with most people.'

'I doubt they would invite just anybody to their ranch in Nevada for the weekend,' Mac said.

'I don't know what you're thinking about, Mac,' she muttered. 'You can't get any deeper into this pretence; it isn't right.'

'Oh, come on. It's such a tiny deception, it's harmless. And it's worked wonders. J.B. was slapping me on the back last night, telling me he'd take me out to the site for the casino at the weekend. It sounds like the job is practically mine.'

'Well, I'm sorry, Mac. But you'll have to swing the rest of it without me.' She straightened her knife and fork on her plate. She couldn't eat anything else.

'I'll pay you for your time,' Mac said suddenly. 'And I'll pay you well. Just think of it as if you're an actress.'

Melissa felt colour seeping up under her skin. 'I don't believe you just said that.' Her voice was very low, very controlled and dignified. 'I'm not some kind of...hooker, Mac.' She glared at him. 'And I'm no actress. I'm not doing it. That's my final word.'

The waitress came back to the table to clear their plates away. 'Did you folks enjoy your meal?' she asked anxiously, looking at Melissa's plate of food.

'Yes, we did,' Melissa assured her. 'We're just in a hurry to leave. Do you think you could bring us the bill?'

'Sure.'

Melissa avoided looking at Mac as they waited. She felt her heart thumping unevenly against her chest. She was horrified by his suggestion, and hurt, and she couldn't wait to get out of here now.

'I didn't mean to suggest for one moment that you were some kind of hooker,' he said in a low, steady voice. 'I don't know why you are being so virulent, Melissa. It's a weekend away. We'll be flying on the company jet to a luxurious ranch. It'll be fun. We can go into Vegas and roll the dice.'

'Or roll in the sack?' Melissa said dryly. 'You haven't even stopped to think about this, have you, Mac? J.B. and Nancy think we are a couple, so where do you think they'll expect us to sleep at their ranch?' She looked at him with a raised eyebrow. 'Hmm, have you thought about that?' Before he could answer her, she continued, 'I'll tell you where. In the same double bed.'

He shrugged. 'Just because we share the same room together doesn't mean I'm going to jump on you,' he answered with equal sarcasm. 'I can exercise restraint, you know.'

Their eyes met mutinously across the table. Suddenly Melissa found herself wondering if she could say the same thing. The notion dismayed her, embarrassed her. 'I wouldn't want to be in the same room as you, Mac.' She spoke impulsively and vehemently.

She watched his eyebrows rise. He looked startled by her words and she wondered, suddenly, if she had struck a blow to his male ego. Good, she thought cheerfully. He deserved to accept some small blow to his pride after bringing her out here under false pretences.

'Why not?' he asked quietly.

'You're not my type for a start,' she continued airily.

'Well, as I'm not expecting anything from you other than good acting abilities, that's not a problem, is it?' His tone was brusque now.

'It doesn't matter what you are expecting, the answer is still no.'

Mac stared at her across the table. He felt truly irritated by her. Why he should be so annoyed, he didn't know. A few hours ago he had held no notion of asking her to do this for him; now he felt as if it was a matter of utmost importance to get her to agree to it.

'OK, here's the deal.' He leaned across the table and fixed her with a level, brooding stare. 'You help me get my career on track, I pay all the aftercare hospital bills for your mother.'

Melissa's eyes widened.

'It will pay better than bar work, I assure you,' he said wryly. 'One weekend with me in Nevada and your problems will be solved.'

'Do you know how much you're talking about?' she asked unsteadily.

'I've got a good idea.' In sharp contrast to her, he sounded perfectly composed. 'Just send me the bills.'

Melissa was stunned at such an offer, maybe even flattered and tempted for just a moment as she thought about her mother. Then distaste flooded through her. Did he think she could be bought?

'You think about it,' Mac said quietly. 'I'll give you until tomorrow evening. Then I'll have to give J.B. a definite answer.'

CHAPTER SEVEN

THE heat of the sun was fading, but the heat of indecision inside Melissa was intensifying with every moment that ticked by. She tried to just concentrate on the garden, but she was subconsciously listening for the sound of Mac's car in the driveway. He would be home soon, and he would expect an answer. She didn't know what to do.

She stood back and surveyed her day's work. The garden was coming together now. She had been creating a water feature that was to sit by a shady arbour. Tomorrow she would plant up the beds around it.

Meanwhile she had to decide what answer to give Mac.

She had lain awake last night thinking about the situation. Deep down, his offer of a weekend away was not unappealing. But she wanted it to be for real. Melissa wanted him to be as attracted to her as she was to him. His suggestion to make it all a businesslike arrangement hurt.

Of course, she had no earthly right to be hurt. Mac had never really led her on. All he was concerned about was his work. This was a problem she had created for herself. If she were to think in practical terms, she would just see his offer as the answer to her worries about her mother. Trouble was, she found it very hard to be pragmatic around Mac Schofield. When she was in his company she yearned for something more. She was so captivated by him that it scared her. Unrequited lust, that was what it was, she told herself, trying to see things in a humorous light. Mac had told her that just because they had to share a room that didn't mean he would pounce on her. The last thing she wanted was to lie in bed next to Mac Schofield in a purely platonic relationship. In a way, it was an insult.

Even though she was desperately worried about her mother and really needed the help, she had made up her mind to turn down Mac's offer by the time daylight had crept into her bedroom this morning. It was a matter of dignity.

Then the flowers had arrived. Armfuls of white daisies and red roses. There had been no message accompanying the flowers, just Mac's name in a simple scrawl on the bottom of the card.

The gesture had touched her. Made her think again.

When Mac walked around the side of the house a little while later, he saw her sitting by the pool, her face a picture of concentration.

The last rays of golden sun slanted over her, highlighting the red tones in the darkness of her hair. She wore a pair of khaki baggy trousers and a black top which was very brief and showed the curves of her breasts and her tiny waist in a way that quickened his pulses.

He frowned to himself, angry for noticing. But it was hard not to; she was very attractive. She turned as she heard his approach.

'Hi.' He smiled, then glanced at the water feature. 'That's nice.'

'Thanks. It's only what you agreed on with Kurt.'

Her eyes slipped over him. He was wearing a suit. It did wonderful things for him. She felt the heat of attraction rise even higher inside. To quell it, she had to turn away from him, pretend to be busy.

'Thank you for the flowers,' she said quietly.

'I suppose they are a bit like sending candy to someone with a candy store,' he said, 'but I really wanted you to know that I never meant to insult you, or imply in any way anything immoral or improper.' He crouched down beside her. 'I'm truly sorry that you took it that way.'

The genuine warmth in his voice made her melt. She looked at him and tried to find a calm and indifferent voice to answer him.

'Please forgive me, Melissa.' He reached out and touched her face. 'Can we start again?'

She smiled. 'Well...when you put it like that.'

'Good.' He smiled back. For a moment they just looked at each other. Then Mac straightened.

'Have you nearly finished for the day? Will you come in and have coffee with me?'

She nodded. 'I won't be long.'

She listened to the sound of his footsteps going towards the house, her heart racing. If he asked her again to go away with him for the weekend, what should she do?

The only way she could agree to the situation was if she could drum up a protective barrier from somewhere. She had managed it yesterday, when she had told him he wasn't her type. But yesterday she had been annoyed with him and it had been easy to lie, to try and bluff her way out of feeling hurt.

If she accepted his proposition, and she couldn't maintain a dignified aloofness, she was going to be completely humiliated.

Slowly she made her way up to the house. She knocked on the back door and heard him shout at her to come in.

After taking off her boots and her gloves, she stepped into the kitchen. Patricia must have been baking—there was a warm smell of cinnamon in the air, and on some racks some cookies were spread out to cool.

Mac was on the phone, his back to her, Lucy balanced on his hip. 'All right, Kay, just pop over later,' he was saying.

He turned and saw Melissa and mouthed, 'Sorry.'

Lucy smiled at her and held out a hand to go to her.

'Well, don't worry about it. You know what these advertising guys are like.' He continued his conversation. Lucy swayed sideways in his arms in a determined effort to get to Melissa, wriggling her legs.

Mac covered the mouthpiece, 'You're popular,' he said with a grin.

'I'll take her if you like,' Melissa whispered.

He nodded and handed the wriggling child over. 'Sorry, Kay, what did you say? No, nobody, just Lucy.'

Melissa frowned. Had he just referred to her as 'nobody'?

'Look, don't worry about it, honey. Of course I'll look at the plans for you if you want. But I'm sure there's no need; you'll have done a first-rate job; you always do. OK, see you later.' He put down the phone.

'I'm nobody, huh?' Melissa couldn't help but make the barbed remark.

He frowned. 'I meant nobody she knows. Sorry, Melissa. That was Kay; she's in a bit of a state about some work she's done. Some ignoramus is threatening to sue her. Says she hasn't done something right.'

'How do you know she hasn't?' Melissa asked lightly.

Mac laughed. 'You don't know Kay like I do. She's meticulous about her work.'

'Really.' He'd called her 'honey', Melissa noted, and he seemed very impressed with her. She would never have guessed in a million years that he was talking about an *ex*-wife. 'It's nice that you're still so friendly.'

'Well, she is Lucy's mother, when all's said and done.'

Patricia came into the room. 'I'm off now, Mac,' she said cheerily. 'See you tomorrow.'

'OK, thanks, Patricia.'

The silence in the kitchen seemed very intense after the other woman had left. Even Lucy's gurgling sounds of contentment did little to lighten the tense atmosphere.

'Let's go and sit in the lounge, shall we?' Mac said,

picking up the tray of coffee and turning to lead the way. 'The garden is progressing well now, isn't it?' he said conversationally.

Melissa was relieved that he wasn't going to mention the weekend straight away. It gave her a little more time to compose her thoughts. 'Yes, but we do need to talk about the rest of the planting.'

'I'll leave the planting and the design entirely in your hands, Melissa.' He sat on the settee and poured the coffee. 'Pretend it's your garden.'

'Like you want me to pretend to be your girlfriend.' Her eyes held his steadily. There was silence for a second, and in it Melissa could hear her heart thumping against her chest. 'We'll have to take care we don't get carried away with all this make-believe.'

He didn't answer her immediately, and she suddenly wished she hadn't said that. 'I mean, it could end up a costly experience. Plants are expensive.'

'I'm not worried about the money.'

'Kurt will be pleased,' Melissa said. She sat opposite him in the chair, Lucy on her knee.

'If I get this contract with J.B., you can gold-plate the garden as far as I'm concerned,' he murmured with a grin.

He looked across at her, one eyebrow raised in question. 'Will you come to J.B.'s ranch this weekend?'

'I might do—' Lucy reached up, grabbed a handful of her hair and gave it a sharp tug, causing her to break off abruptly in mid-sentence. 'Ow!'

Mac frowned. 'Lucy, that's naughty; stop it.'

Instead of stopping Lucy pulled at her hair again and laughed, as if she had just discovered a wonderful new game. Melissa reached up to try and untangle her hair from around the little girl's hands; Lucy had a surprisingly strong grip on her.

'Lucy! What's gotten into you?' Mac got up from the settee to come and help. 'Sorry, Melissa.'

He knelt down beside her chair, leaned in close to unwind the baby's fingers from the silky tresses. 'Come on, Lucy, stop this,' he murmured impatiently.

His head was very close to Melissa's. It was brought even closer as Lucy gave one last almighty tug on her hair, causing her to jerk forward, and her forehead to bang against his.

'Ow!' Melissa found herself staring right into his eyes, their lips centimetres apart.

'Are you OK?' He raised his hand to touch her head. She couldn't answer him. She felt breathless suddenly.

They were so close that she noticed the faint dark shadow around his firm square jaw. His velvety dark eyes had flecks of gold in them.

His hand stroked her head. A tingling feeling started in the pit of her stomach and worked its spiralling fingers through her, followed by a surge of desire akin to the hollow feeling of hunger. She tried to dismiss it, but it wouldn't go away.

His hand moved to cup the side of her face. She wanted him to kiss her. She felt herself swaying closer towards him.

Then Lucy got tired of her game and let go of her hair to try and wriggle off her knee between them, pushing them apart.

'Are you OK?' he asked, moving even farther back from her, and she wondered suddenly if she had imagined the forceful, compelling sensuality that had just flowed between them.

'Yes.' She rubbed at her head and avoided looking at him.

Mac glared down at Melissa, annoyed with himself. He had wanted to kiss her. The feeling had been incredible. Fiercely he reminded himself that he wanted to avoid complications in his life, not create them. How could he persuade Melissa that she would be perfectly safe sharing a bedroom with him, when he found it hard keeping his hands off her in the lounge?

He moved slowly away from her back to his seat. 'Now, where were we?'

Her eyes, wide and shimmering, held his. She couldn't remember what they had been talking about.

Lucy, totally oblivious to the havoc she had started, toddled around the room, found a small box of soft toys that had been left for her in a corner, and started to tip them all out onto the floor.

'Ah, yes…' he smiled '…I was trying to convince you how much I need you this weekend.'

'Were you?' She shrugged, trying to pretend a nonchalant indifference that she honestly didn't feel. 'You know, I can't help feeling that you've made a big mistake not asking your ex-wife to play out this pretence.'

Mac's eyebrows lifted. 'Why?'

Melissa shrugged. 'You sounded very at ease with her and—'

'I'm very at ease with you,' he murmured softly.

'Now you're trying to flatter me into agreeing, aren't you?' she maintained humorously, trying to ignore the way her senses reacted to him. 'Let me tell you, Mac, I'm not that easily duped. Going away with you for the weekend isn't about you…liking me, it's about you getting a job, so you don't have to sweet-talk me.'

'Well, I've tried bribery, and it doesn't seem to be getting me too far either,' he grinned.

Lucy toddled back to Melissa's chair and held up a pink elephant for her inspection. 'Is that for me?' Melissa asked with a smile, taking it from her. 'Thank you.' The child gave a dimpled grin before rushing unsteadily back to her toy box.

'I'd really appreciate it if you would agree to this weekend, Melissa,' Mac continued. 'And I assure you that even though we will have to share a room, I'll sleep on the floor.

There will be no need for you to worry about anything on that score.'

She shrugged. 'Damn right you'd sleep on the floor.'

'Is that a yes?' he asked hopefully.

She hesitated. She wanted it to be yes, wanted to spend some more time with him. 'Well, I was thinking about what you said—you know, about my opening up too much to Nancy and J.B.' She kept her voice carefully light. 'Maybe I did. I'm not really the reserved type. I like to be sociable—it's part of my nature.'

'There's nothing wrong with that,' Mac said.

'No. But maybe you had a point…a very *small* point,' she emphasised. 'Maybe I did unwittingly create this situation…this invitation…by being too chatty, or enthusiastic…whatever. So perhaps I should help you out.' She felt quite proud of herself. She sounded casual, no hint of any personal interest at all. 'And anyway, I've never been to Vegas.'

He smiled at her. It was a smile that made her emotions contradict her nonchalant words very forcefully.

'Thank you,' he said gently.

She nodded. 'But I don't want any payment, Mac.'

'Oh, no, that offer still holds…'

She felt herself squirming. The talk of money was all so distasteful, so mercenary. 'I don't want you to pay me.' As he seemed about to protest again, she cut across him hurriedly. 'That's final, Mac. It's my last word on the subject.' She had no intention of taking his money, no matter how desperate she was to help her mother. She just couldn't do that.

Lucy pulled another toy out of her box and held it up. 'Issa,' she called. 'Issa, look.'

'She's calling you,' Mac said in surprise.

Melissa looked across at the child. She looked so adorable in her little yellow romper suit, the expression on her baby face one of complete satisfaction as she gained

Melissa's attention. 'Look,' she said, waggling a blue knitted cat. 'Omas cat.'

Melissa glanced at Mac, looking for clarification. 'Thomas, the cat,' he translated for her.

'Oh.' Melissa smiled. 'I see.'

Lucy came hurtling back across the room, holding the cat by the tail.

'A good job it's not a real one,' Melissa said, laughing.

Lucy held the cat out to her triumphantly. 'Mine cat.'

'It's lovely, darling.' Melissa reached to take it, but Lucy didn't let go.

'She loves that cat,' Mac said with a shake of his head. 'Heaven knows why; it's a bit tattered now. On the last of its nine lives, so to speak.'

Lucy climbed up on the chair and sat on her knee, shoving the cat farther up towards her face for closer inspection.

Its long tail was loose and the stitching around the ears was starting to fray. The embroidered eyes and mouth were a bit worn as well.

'Omas is definitely a bit battle-weary.' Melissa grinned. 'But beautiful, just the same.'

Lucy hugged the cat and grinned up at her, as if pleased with her verdict. Melissa wanted to hug her as closely as she was hugging that toy. There was something about the little girl that brought out those tender, responsive feelings in her.

Mac reached for his coffee and tried not to notice how Lucy had taken to Melissa. She had never once tried to say Tara's name, and she had never climbed onto Tara's knee either. If she had, Tara would probably have complained that she had rumpled her skirt. Tara had always been very concerned with keeping her image perfect.

He sipped his coffee, annoyed with himself for thinking like this. He wanted to keep all thoughts about Melissa strictly on a business level. Yet, again and again, he kept remembering the way she had responded to his kiss the other night. He had wanted to take the passion further. He had wanted to kiss her a few minutes ago. She was a walking time bomb. The sweetness in her response, the warmth in her eyes when she looked at him were hard to resist.

He reminded himself of her words to him yesterday, her unequivocal statement that he wasn't really her type. He frowned at the memory. Who was her type? Simon Wesley?

'I'll phone Nancy tonight,' he told her abruptly. 'Thank her for the party and tell her we will look forward to the weekend.'

'OK.' Melissa shrugged.

He watched as Lucy relinquished her beloved Omas into her hands, how she giggled with delight as Melissa played peek-a-boo with the toy.

'I'll mention to her that she should ask Simon about her plant,' he continued nonchalantly. 'That way you won't have to go through the ordeal of phoning him yourself.'

'It wouldn't have been an ordeal,' she said with a smile. She was well over Simon. The thought of ringing him didn't bother her in the least.

'Yes, well, it might be better if you don't speak to him for a while, just until you and I are established as a couple at the weekend. We don't want anything complicating the situation, do we?'

'I don't see how my talking to Simon about a plant could complicate things.'

'If he asks you out and you're tempted to go, that's a big complication,' Mac said smoothly.

That wouldn't be a complication, it would be a disaster, Melissa thought, with a wry twist of her lips. She wouldn't date Simon Wesley again if he offered her the sun, moon and stars. 'Well, if it helps put your mind at ease about the weekend.' Her voice held an abrasive note. It didn't particularly boost her ego to be reminded that Mac's only concern about her dating Simon was the threat to their pretence.

'Great.' He smiled at her.

She looked back down at the child on her knee. Lucy was watching her eagerly, waiting for their game to resume.

'You seem to have gained a fan,' Mac remarked.

'Yes.' She glanced over at him, her eyes piercingly direct. 'That will make things much easier at the weekend as well, I suppose.'

'Undoubtedly.'

It was crazy to feel hurt. She had agreed to this venture. Knew the score. Suddenly she had this horrible feeling that she was opening herself up to a lot of heartache.

Wasn't she the one who had vowed never to get involved with a man again unless she was certain that he wanted her as much as she wanted him? No more half measures, no more broken hearts?

'Any other little rules of deception you'd like to set down before we go off for this weekend?' she asked him in a brittle tone.

'Sorry?' He looked at her blankly.

'Well, I'm not to ring Simon. Presumably I'm not to be too friendly with Nancy, or too chatty with J.B.? Is there anything else you'd like me to avoid?'

Mac met her eyes over Lucy's head. Looking at me like that could be pretty hazardous, he thought hazily. Her hair was in glossy disarray around her shoulders. Her eyes sparkled with a fierce light that was, at one and the same time, spirited yet filled with a feminine vulnerability that caught his breath. 'I don't think so.' He shrugged. 'In fairness, are there any little rules that you'd like to give me?' he asked, trying to think logically, and not about how desirable he found her.

'Yes. Just don't touch me if you can possibly help it.'

Mac blinked in surprise. 'I told you I'd sleep on the floor.'

'Yes… well, just see that you do. I don't want you thinking you can take advantage of me.'

'The thought never crossed my mind.' Mac glared at her.

She glared back at him. 'As long as we are under no illusions, that's fine.'

'Fine,' he agreed. He stood up and walked to the sideboard to pour himself a stiff drink. Suddenly he felt as if he might need one.

Melissa leaned her head back against the cushions and cursed herself. She had gone completely overboard. He'd know now that she was interested in him. It had stood out a mile that she was hurt by his cool, aloof manner.

'Fancy a whisky?' He turned and held up the bottle.

Quickly she opened her eyes and smiled politely. 'No, thanks. I'd better get off.'

He watched as she kissed Lucy and put her down gently on the floor. Her top was twisted, and he could see a provocative glimpse of a golden-brown, slender midriff before she adjusted it.

'See you tomorrow, then.' She smiled at him.

'Well, if I don't see you before then I'll see you Friday afternoon,' he said coolly.

Melissa's lips set in a determined line as she made her way towards the front door. She'd teach him to play cool with her. She intended to use every womanly wile at her disposal to get Mac to fall for her this weekend, if it was the last thing she did. Then she would thank him, ever so politely on Sunday, and walk away. The thought gave her immense pleasure for a moment.

Mac opened the front door for her. He caught hold of her arm as she made to walk past him. 'Hey.' His voice was gentle. 'Thanks once again, Melissa. I really do appreciate this.'

Melissa looked from him to the child in his arms. 'You're welcome.'

He smiled, a smile that lit up the darkness of his eyes with a warmth that seemed to heat Melissa through to her bones.

But then, of course, if he really did fall for her, if there was any prospect of a relationship growing between them, it would be crazy not to give it a chance, she thought as she turned away from him.

CHAPTER EIGHT

MELISSA glanced out of the plane window at the parched desert below. The anticipation that had been bubbling inside her all week at the thought of this trip to Vegas had suddenly become tinged with apprehension. Now that it was Friday and she was actually on her way, second thoughts had started to creep in.

It was one thing telling herself in theory that she was going to make Mac fall for her, and quite another putting it into practice. She was going to be sharing a bedroom, for two nights, with a man that she was seriously attracted to, a man who really only wanted her here to further his career. When she actually started to rationalise the situation, it seemed like a recipe for disaster. What basis was there for even thinking she stood half a chance with Mac? Was she deluding herself?

Melissa looked down at the sleeping baby on her knee. Since take-off Lucy had been out for the count—first of all on Mac's knee and then, as he wanted to read some reports that J.B. had sent for him, she had been gently transferred over to hers.

She studied the little face intently: the long sooty eyelashes against the creamy baby skin, the rosy cheeks, the small rosebud lips pouted softly in sleep.

'Do you want me to take her from you?' Mac asked, interrupting her thoughts. 'Is she getting heavy?'

'No, she's fine,' Melissa assured him. In fact, she was extremely comfortable. The seats were wide and spacious and Lucy was positioned snugly against her.

The flight attendant came down with a bottle of champagne and two glasses. 'With Mr Bradford's compliments,' she said as she put the ice bucket next to Mac. 'Enjoy yourselves!'

Melissa's eyebrows rose. 'J.B. is certainly pulling out all the stops for us,' she said. 'A whole plane to ourselves, and now champagne.'

'Yes. I'm hoping it means my job with the firm is a certainty, especially as the reading material he has left for me is the report on this new casino.' He reached and poured her a glass of the champagne.

'Aren't you having one?' she asked as she accepted it and noticed he wasn't pouring himself one.

'No, I want to keep a clear head.'

He returned his attention to the report in front of him, a frown of concentration marring the smoothly good-looking face.

Melissa looked down at the golden bubbles in the drink. She wanted to tell him that it was no fun drinking champagne on her own, but she didn't dare. Mac's deep preoccupation with work didn't inspire remarks like that. She wasn't supposed to be here having fun.

Melissa sipped her champagne, leaned her head back against the leather seats and tried to recapture even a quarter of the optimism she had been feeling earlier.

She had thought that J.B. and Nancy would be on the flight with them, but apparently they were already in Nevada and would be picking them up from the airport. Her joy at finding that they were to be alone on the plane had quickly dwindled as Mac had immersed himself in his report. She wondered if the rest of the weekend would be the same.

'Oh, I almost forgot.' Mac's voice made her eyes jerk open. 'I meant to give you this before we left for the airport.'

He put a small jewellery box on the table next to her champagne glass.

'What is it?' she asked suspiciously.

'Open it up and see.'

Cautiously she lifted the lid. The most beautiful square-cut diamond ring winked at her from red velvet. It took her breath away. 'It's gorgeous, Mac!'

'I thought it might help convince people that we are...together.' He reached across and took it out of the box. Then gently picked up her left hand from where it rested around Lucy, to push it firmly down on her third finger. 'There, that's better. I noticed Simon looking to see if you had a ring on when we were at that party last Saturday. If he happens to be out at the ranch while we are there, that should answer any questions he has.'

'Do you think he will be there?' she asked in surprise.

'I don't know. J.B. mentioned there was a big meeting this weekend in Vegas with the board of directors for the casino. As Simon has been retained to plan the gardens, he could be there.' Mac watched as she admired the ring on her finger, turning it to catch the sunlight so that its icy beauty glittered with a myriad of spectacular colours. 'I take it you haven't spoken to him?' he asked suddenly.

'I told you I wouldn't.'

'I know you did. But I just wondered if he had tried to contact you again?'

'No.' She dragged her eyes away from the beauty of the ring. 'Mac, you didn't buy this especially to impress Simon Wesley, did you? It must have cost a fortune.'

'No, of course not.' Mac returned his attention to the papers in front of him, as if he had suddenly lost interest in the conversation. 'It's just to make things a bit more authentic, that's all. Look on it as a stage prop.'

Melissa sensed that he wanted her to drop the subject, but she couldn't. She was overcome with curiosity. 'Is it real?'

He glanced over at her with a glint of amusement in his eyes. 'Does it matter?'

'Well, yes. If it's real, I'll guard it with my life and

hand it back to you as soon as we get on the plane to come home.' She would have to be careful with it, she mused, twisting it thoughtfully. It was a bit too big for her.

'You can keep it, Melissa,' he said, returning his attention to his papers. 'Now, if you don't mind, I just want to finish reading this before we land.'

'Fine.' She looked down at the ring again. If he was allowing her to keep it, it had to be a fake. 'It's amazing how good these cubic zircons are. I'd swear that it's real,' she said incredulously.

Mac rattled his papers impatiently.

'Sorry,' she murmured. 'I'll shut up now.'

Mac glared down at the papers in front of him. He didn't particularly want to read the damn report. He wanted to push it all away and sit looking at Melissa.

The ring sparkled as the light caught it. He glanced sideways at her. She had lovely hands and nails—well manicured, very feminine. He had noticed how she took special care of her hands, how she wore gloves when she was working, how soft and small they were when he took hold of them.

He turned swiftly back to the report. If he didn't stop thinking about Melissa in this way, the weekend would be a disaster. This was business, he told himself firmly, and the ring was to make things easier—keep Simon Wesley at bay for a start.

Despite the admonishment, he still couldn't concentrate on the report. Out of the corner of his eye, he was aware of her every movement. She admired the ring for a few more moments, then took another sip of her champagne, before leaning her head back against the seat and closing her eyes again. She was probably tired, he thought. He knew she had worked until four-thirty this afternoon, before going home to her apartment to get ready for the journey.

He glanced across at her again. The pale blue dress she

wore was light and summery. Her dark hair was resting against Lucy's blonde curls. They both looked the picture of contentment. He couldn't tear his attention away from them.

Suddenly her eyes opened and he found himself looking straight into them. 'I thought you were asleep.' Mac tried very hard to keep his voice level, but he was aware that it had taken on a husky overtone.

'I think I was for a minute.' She sounded disorientated.

He glanced past her out of the window. 'There's a beautiful sunset,' he observed, trying to distract her from the fact that he had been watching her.

She turned and looked out. The sky was streaked with vivid blood-orange against the deep purple of encroaching darkness. There was something profoundly inspiring about the scene. She leaned forward to take a better look. The lights of Las Vegas were coming into view, a glittering oasis in the vast emptiness of the desert.

Her eyes sparkled with excitement as she looked back at him. 'I can see Vegas.'

He leaned across her to look out of the window. But he was more aware of her than the view. The tantalising fragrance of her perfume, the touch of her arm against his. 'Yes, we'll be landing soon.' Mac sat back and looked down at the papers on his table. Who the hell was he kidding? he thought angrily. This wasn't just business. He wanted to kiss her, hold her, make very passionate love to her.

He had been deluding himself that he could keep his intentions strictly contained towards business. He had lied to himself, and, worse, he had lied to her. Realisation was sharp: he had wanted to take her away for this weekend. Wanted to share the bedroom with her.

Mac was stunned at how he had been able to deceive himself, talk himself into believing that his motives were purely business ones. Why the hell he had done it, he didn't know. It was as if he had seized the excuse to hide behind and had firmly stuck to it. But in fact, it was seduction that was uppermost in his mind.

At least he was being honest with himself now, before it was too late. Whatever the reason, out of decency, he had to maintain the pretence that all he was interested in was gaining this contract. At all costs he had to keep his distance when they were alone together tonight.

Melissa sat in the back of the car with Lucy and Nancy. Mac was up front next to J.B. They had landed at McCarran Airport about fifteen minutes ago. Now J.B. was pointing out the spectacular hotels along the strip as he drove them back to his ranch.

There was no doubt that it was an exciting city. Pulsating, gyrating light burst vibrantly onto the streets. Dancing waterfalls, exploding volcanoes, pirate ships firing cannons; it was all happening down here. There was a replica of the Eiffel Tower, a whole section of the New York skyline, complete with the Statue of Liberty.

'Fabulous, isn't it?' Nancy said. 'If you and Mac want to come down here tomorrow for a night on the town, J.B. and I will babysit for you.'

'We wouldn't dream of imposing on you, Nancy,' Mac said quickly from up front.

'We really wouldn't mind,' Nancy said earnestly. 'Would we, J.B.?'

'Certainly not.' J.B. slowed the car at another junction. 'That's the site for the new casino, Mac,' he said, pointing left. 'You can't see much in the dark, obviously, but I'll bring you down tomorrow morning for a closer look. Then you may as well sit in on the board meeting tomorrow afternoon.'

'Here we go again,' Nancy said in an aside to Melissa. 'Work, work and more work. You and I can have some fun tomorrow anyway; let them bury themselves in the business. We'll do some serious shopping.'

'Good idea.' Melissa smiled at the woman. But deep down she was thinking about Mac.

When she had opened her eyes and found him watching her on the plane, she had felt a fierce tug of attraction flare between them. She had thought it was mutual. It had filled her with exhilaration. Now she was wondering if she had imagined it. He had hardly said two words to her since.

Of course, there hadn't been much chance to talk once they had met up with J.B. and Nancy in the terminal but, all the same, she felt as if he had pulled shutters even more closely down around him. There was a definite distant look in his dark eyes.

The lights of the strip were left behind and the darkness of the desert closed around them as they took the highway out of town.

'Won't be long now,' Nancy told her, looking at the sleeping baby in Melissa's arms. 'You'll be glad to get her settled.'

'She's been remarkably good,' Melissa said. 'She's slept all the way, more or less.'

'I hope that doesn't mean she won't sleep tonight,' Mac said. 'You could be regretting inviting us, Nancy, when Lucy's wails are splitting the peaceful night air.'

'I don't think so.' Nancy laughed. 'Anyway, even if she howls the place down, we won't hear her. We've put you and Melissa in the family wing at the far side of the house. My daughter and son-in-law usually occupy it when they are here. But they can't make it this weekend.'

J.B. turned the car through an imposing-looking driveway, over the rattle of a cattle grid. Lucy stirred in Melissa's arms and gave a little cry.

'Right on her cue,' Melissa smiled. She rocked the baby gently. 'Hush, sweetheart, nearly there now,' she soothed.

The ranch came into view up ahead. It was a large

L-shaped building, all on one level, with golden, welcoming lights spilling from its windows. J.B. pulled the car around to the back of the house, and they got out.

'Wow, it's hot,' Melissa said as the heat hit her in a blast.

'Wait until the sun comes up,' Nancy said with a smile. 'Then you'll know what heat is. Hope you brought your swimsuit, Melissa. We have a pool and a Jacuzzi. In fact, after you've settled Lucy, why don't you have a dip before dinner? This is the perfect time of day to be in the pool.'

'You girls go on ahead,' Mac said. 'If you don't mind, I'm going to have another read through that report, J.B., if I'm to sit in on that meeting tomorrow. I want to be sure of my facts.'

'Yes, by all means.' J.B. took their overnight cases from the trunk of the car. 'We'll put these in your room, then go through to my study. I have some other literature on the project that you should find interesting.'

Melissa followed Nancy into the house. It was built to a very modern design, mostly open-plan. The kitchen was circled by a white breakfast bar which separated it from the morning room. Nancy led the way down a long hallway and opened a door at the end. 'Here we are. Make yourselves at home,' she said.

The stylish bedroom was dominated by the most enormous four-poster bed Melissa had ever seen. It was decorated in tropical lime-green with toning accents of navy blue. Sliding patio doors led out to the pool area. Melissa pulled back the blinds to look out, and could see the turquoise water illuminated by underwater lights, shimmering invitingly.

'There's an *en suite* through here.' Nancy opened another door into a white and gold bathroom. 'And a cot for Lucy through here.' She opened another door into a small annexe which was just big enough for a cot and a chair.

'I'll leave you to get organised. Feel free to go into the kitchen and get yourself anything you need.'

'Thanks, Nancy.' Melissa sat on the bed and put Lucy down beside her. The little girl seemed wide awake now and was taking in her surroundings with interest.

'That's a lovely ring,' Nancy remarked suddenly as Melissa moved her hand and the light glittered over it.

'Yes. Mac gave it to me on the flight over here today.' As soon as she had made the reply she wondered if she had said the right thing. Maybe Mac had wanted her to pretend that he had given her the ring ages ago.

'You've just got engaged!' Nancy shrieked with delight. 'Oh, Melissa, how romantic. Why didn't you tell me straight away? I'll put some champagne on ice. This is cause for a celebration.'

Now Melissa knew for sure that her answer had been a mistake. Mac certainly wouldn't want this kind of fuss and neither did she. 'No…really, Nancy, there's no need—'

'Of course there's a need!' Nancy cut across her. 'You must celebrate in style.'

'What are we celebrating?' Mac asked as he came into the room with their luggage.

'Your engagement of course.' Nancy smiled. 'It's wonderful news, Mac; I'm so pleased for you.'

'Melissa's told you, then?' he murmured, looking across at her.

Melissa felt like cringing as their eyes met. She wondered if he was annoyed with her. If he was, he was hiding it well behind that calm, cool exterior.

'Of course she told me. That dazzler of a ring has near blinded me.' Nancy moved towards the door. 'I'll leave you two love birds alone.'

The door closed behind her, leaving an awkward silence in the room.

'I'm sorry, Mac,' she said as he made no attempt to say anything. 'I didn't set out to tell her that we'd just got engaged. She noticed the ring. Have I made a dreadful blunder?'

'We could have done without the fuss. Nancy will be cracking open the champagne now, and I feel enough of a fraud as it is.'

'I am sorry.' Her eyes seemed a very intense blue as she looked up at him earnestly. 'I'm not very good at deception. The truth just came tumbling out of my mouth before I had time to stop and think. I didn't know what to say to her.'

Lucy distracted them both as, tired of inactivity, she decided she wanted to get down from the bed, and turned herself so that she could slide over the edge onto the floor. Melissa caught hold of the wiggling little body before she could escape. 'Oh, no, you don't,' she said, giving the little girl a kiss and sitting her on her knee.

Mac frowned. She looked so right sitting there holding his daughter. Why was that? And why did he feel so damn helpless when she turned those big violet-blue eyes on him? No woman had ever had this effect on him before. It was as if she had some secret power over him, some secret spell. It made him most uneasy.

He turned away, impatient with himself, and lifted his case up onto one of the chests of drawers to open it.

'So, am I forgiven?' she asked briskly, making a determined effort to eliminate the atmosphere of tension.

'Forgiven?' He glanced over at her, hardly able to remember what they were talking about. 'Forgiven for telling the truth?' He shook his head. 'Now you're making me feel like a total charlatan.' His eyes moved over her. She had a truly unique personality, warm and delightful. He stifled the emotion he felt and turned away. 'The whole thing is my fault. I shouldn't have given you that ring this afternoon.' He started to take Lucy's things from the case. 'We'll just have to bluff our way through it.'

'I suppose so.' She got up from the bed, and carried Lucy over to stand beside him.

He could smell the evocative hints of her perfume.

'Can I give you a hand?' she asked.

He glanced sideways at her. 'No, everything's under control,' he murmured, wishing that were indeed the case. She was having the strangest effect on him. Even the dress she wore, which wasn't overtly sexy, seemed a total distraction. 'I'm going to bath Lucy and change her into her pyjamas.'

She wasn't needed, in other words, Melissa thought. Unperturbed, she carried on. 'Well, how about if I organise some supper for her? Do you think she will be hungry?'

'I don't think so. She ate quite a lot earlier, didn't she...?' Mac hesitated. 'Maybe you could warm some milk up for her? I'm trying to wean her off bottles, but she still likes one at bedtime.'

'Just ordinary milk?'

'Yes.' Mac took out a plastic bottle from the case and handed it over to her. 'Thanks, Melissa,' he said, taking Lucy from her in exchange.

Why did she feel as if she had just been dismissed? Melissa wondered as she headed out of the room. Or was she just being sensitive?

She found Nancy in the kitchen, preparing a salad. 'Would it be all right if I heat some milk up for Lucy?' she asked.

'Of course.' Nancy opened the fridge and brought out a carton. 'I was planning on having a barbecue out by the pool tonight, but now that I know it's such a special evening for you I wish I'd arranged something more flamboyant.'

'A barbecue will be lovely, Nancy. And please don't go to any trouble on our account.'

'It's no trouble.' She poured the milk into the saucepan and turned on the hob. 'You and Mac should do something special to mark your engagement. Maybe tomorrow night the two of you can take me up on that offer to babysit. I really wouldn't mind. I have a granddaughter of about the same age as Lucy, and my daughter and her husband usually hit the town when they visit. So I'm well used to it.'

'It's very kind of you.' Melissa didn't know what else to say. She was half tempted by the idea anyway.

'I'll enjoy it. Lucy is a darling baby, so pretty, with those big blue eyes and blonde curls.'

'Yes, she's gorgeous,' Melissa agreed. 'I'm not her real mother,' she felt impelled to explain. 'But I fell instantly in love with her the moment I first set eyes on her.' She frowned to herself. That statement hadn't been a word of a lie, she realised suddenly. She had fallen in love with Lucy. 'I never really thought of myself as the maternal type before,' she said, speaking almost to herself. 'But I must be...'

Nancy laughed. 'You sound as if you've surprised yourself.'

Melissa smiled. 'Here, let me do that for you.' She reached to take the pan of milk, glad of the excuse to change the subject. She took it over to the sink to pour it into the bottle.

'What happened to Mac's first wife?' Nancy asked suddenly.

'They got divorced. I don't know a lot about it. It's something Mac doesn't really like to talk about.'

'She must have been a pretty cold person if she could leave her baby behind.'

Melissa frowned. 'I don't know. I've never met her, and I don't suppose it's fair to judge unless you know all the details.'

'I suppose not,' Nancy agreed. She looked across at Melissa and smiled. 'One thing I can say for certain— Mac's a very lucky man to have met you.'

'I'll second that,' Mac said from behind them.

His voice made them both jump. Melissa found herself colouring bright red as she turned and met his eyes. She wondered how much of their conversation he had overheard. She hoped he hadn't heard her telling Nancy that she had fallen in love with his daughter. She felt foolish, as if she had been caught once again, overstepping the boundary lines he had drawn up.

'I was just coming with the bottle,' she said brightly, trying to carry on as normal. Melissa tested the temperature on the back of her wrist. 'It should be all right for her.'

He reached and took it from her, then smiled at her in a way that made her heart flutter crazily. 'Thanks,' he said softly.

The faint sound of Lucy's crying drifted down the hall, making him turn hurriedly. 'I'd better get this to her before she yells the place down.'

'I hope he didn't hear me talking about his ex-wife,' Nancy said as soon as the door had closed behind him again. 'I didn't hear him come out of the bedroom.'

'Neither did I,' Melissa admitted. 'I don't think he heard us. But it doesn't really matter if he did; we weren't saying anything out of turn.' With difficulty, she tried to compose her thoughts. 'Now, let me give you some help with the preparations for dinner,' she said.

'There's nothing to do, Melissa,' Nancy insisted. 'You go and take a dip in the pool.'

Having lost the battle to be of some help, Melissa wandered out and back to the bedroom. It was silent and empty. She moved to the door of the nursery and peeped in. Mac was sitting in the chair, Lucy on his knee. She was wearing a pair of blue kitten pyjamas and was happily drinking her milk, holding the bottle herself.

Mac looked up and met her eyes. 'I'm going to have a swim,' she said, searching for something to say to excuse herself for barging in.

'OK,' he smiled. 'Hey, Lucy, say goodnight to Melissa.'

Melissa waved at the little girl, and she put her bottle down to wave back.

'Goodnight, sweetheart.' Melissa wanted to go and give her a hug and kiss.

I'm getting too emotionally involved here, she thought warily as she started to turn away.

'Melissa.' Mac's voice stopped her. 'Do you think you could look after Lucy for me tomorrow?'

'Yes, of course,' she answered without hesitation.

'Thanks. J.B. wants to take me down to the building site in the morning and then there's the meeting in the afternoon.'

'That's fine.'

Lucy dropped her bottle on the floor and Melissa went over to pick it up for her. 'There you go, honey.' She crouched down next to the chair and handed it back. 'Does that entitle me to a goodnight kiss?' she asked, tickling her under the chin playfully.

Lucy giggled and then leaned nearer so that Melissa could kiss her. 'You smell of peaches and cream,' Melissa said as she kissed her on the cheek and then on the other cheek. 'Good enough to eat.'

'Peach bubble bath,' Mac informed her. 'She managed to tip the bottle as I was pouring it into the water. We had bubbles everywhere.'

'Sounds as if I missed out on some fun.' Melissa smiled at the little girl, then glanced up at Mac.

There was a very serious light in his dark eyes that stilled the amusement inside her, grounding her. 'You sounded as if you meant that,' he said quietly.

'What, that it sounded like fun?' She sat back on her heels, looking up at him with a frown. 'Well, it did.'

'You meant what you said to Nancy as well, didn't you?' he asked suddenly.

She felt her cheeks growing red. 'What did I say to

Nancy?' she prevaricated, hoping he hadn't heard the start of that conversation.

He smiled. 'You know very well that I'm referring to the way you talked about Lucy.'

Melissa shrugged. She wanted to say that she had just been playing her part, acting—that was all it had been. But one glance at Lucy, who was drinking her milk and watching her with those angelic blue eyes, and she couldn't lie. 'Maybe looking at Lucy makes me think about what I'm missing in my life,' she said instead, evading a straight answer, and giving one that wasn't altogether untrue.

'Did you and Simon plan to have a family?'

'We talked about it,' Melissa said honestly. 'I used to say how much I'd like a little girl.' She thought back for a moment. 'Now that I reflect on those conversations, he was never thrilled about the idea. He used to say that there was time enough to think about that when we'd been married for a few years.'

'Sounds like something Kay would have said.'

'How long were you and Kay together?' Melissa asked curiously.

'We were married for five years, but I'd known her a lot longer than that. We met at college. Like me, she was training to be an architect.'

Lucy finished her bottle and settled herself more comfortably against her father's chest. She was looking sleepy now, her eyes heavy with the effort of trying to keep awake.

Mac stroked her curls back from her face with a gentle hand. He seemed in no hurry to put her down for the evening and Melissa hoped he was going to continue with their conversation. She wanted to know more about his past.

'We qualified at the same time and went to work at the same firm.'

'Was it a coincidence that you both went to work for the same company?' Melissa asked curiously.

'No. Kay admitted later that she applied for the job after she discovered that was where I was going.' He smiled. 'I was flattered. I liked her a lot.' He paused for a moment. 'She was…well, still is…a very beautiful woman.'

Melissa looked away from him. She felt a thrust of jealousy deep inside, and it shocked her. How could she be jealous of a woman she had never met, had never even seen?

'We moved into an apartment together. One of these trendy developments with electric gates and twenty-four-hour security. One bedroom. Very modern, very upmarket. It was her choice. Even right back then, I'd have gone for the two-bedroomed family home.' His lips twisted wryly. 'Sometimes, when I look back, I wonder if I missed the signs; they were there if I'd have looked carefully. But we were testing the waters anyway…so to speak, so it suited, and I went along with it. We were both totally engrossed in our careers, so much so that I think that was the main thing we had in common. She's a very brilliant architect.'

'Beautiful *and* brilliant,' Melissa murmured. 'You sound like you are still in love with her.'

'I did love her,' Mac said quietly. 'Very much.'

Melissa was quite unprepared for the effect that statement had on her. If she had thought she felt jealous a moment ago, it was nothing to the fierce tug of emotion that stirred to life now. She was angry with herself for feeling like that, but she couldn't seem to help it. 'And now?' she asked quietly.

'Now I just feel sad when I think about how things went wrong.' Mac looked down at Lucy. She was fast asleep, her little mouth pouted in a perfect rosebud. 'Especially sad for Lucy. Because Kay just isn't interested in her at all.'

He looked up and met Melissa's eyes, and her jealousy

faded away as if it had never been. Divorce was awful, but it was especially sad when there was a child involved. 'At least Lucy has you,' she said softly. 'One good parent is better than two unhappy ones.'

'I suppose so.' He shrugged. 'I'll do my best for her, that's for sure. I love her very much and I don't regret having her. She's the best thing that's ever happened in my life.'

'Even though she cost you your marriage?'

Mac frowned. 'I think my marriage would have ended anyway. Kay wanted a business partner more than she wanted a husband. Sometimes I feel guilty when I think how I talked her into going ahead with the pregnancy… Don't get me wrong, I desperately wanted Lucy. But the pregnancy wasn't planned and it wasn't right for Kay. She was up for promotion at work; the timing couldn't have been worse. I naively thought that we could work it all out. We weren't short of money. But I realise now that, no matter what our circumstances, it would never have been the right time for Kay. Motherhood just wasn't her thing, and neither, really, was marriage.'

'Is she happy now?'

'I think so. She's immersed in her business and she has a boyfriend, and I think life is as she wants it. As you probably gathered, we're still friends…which is something my mother can't understand,' he added wryly. 'She thinks Kay is very cold. But she isn't. She's just Kay. She never pretended to be anything other than what she is, and my life is richer for knowing her.' He started to get up from the chair very carefully so as not to wake Lucy.

'You are definitely still in love with her,' Melissa observed as she watched him put the baby down in the cot.

'No, I'm not.' He turned and offered her his hand to help her get to her feet.

Her foot had gone stiff from the way she had been sitting on it and she stumbled. He put an arm around her to steady her, and suddenly she found herself very close to him.

She looked up at him and felt her heart starting to beat a very uneven and rapid tattoo.

'I'm really not,' he said again.

She wondered if he was trying to convince himself, or her.

She wanted him to kiss her. Her eyes moved to his mouth which seemed too enticing, too close.

'I suppose we should go outside and see what our hosts are doing,' he said dazedly, trying to make himself move away from her.

'I suppose we should.'

He leaned his head closer and touched his lips against hers. The feeling was warm and sensual. Gently he explored her in a way that created a storm of emotion inside her. She wanted more; she wanted his kiss to deepen, for him to wrap his arms around her and never let her go.

Melissa felt extremely shaken by the feelings as he stepped back.

A knock on the bedroom door disturbed the tense silence between them.

'That will be J.B. He said he'd give me some time to get Lucy settled then bring the rest of the reports for me to look at.' His eyes moved gently over her, noting the high colour on her skin. 'We'll talk about this later, OK?'

CHAPTER NINE

MELISSA rested her head back against the comfortable reclining chair and looked up, noticing how bright the stars were. The intense heat of the night and the silence of the desert were very relaxing. There was a delicious aroma of food drifting in the air, and the only sound was the faint sizzle of steak on the barbecue.

It was a little over an hour since Mac had kissed her. He had been immersed in J.B.'s office ever since. She had swum several lengths of the pool in an attempt to restore some kind of calm in the midst of so many euphoric sensations.

She shouldn't try to read anything into that kiss, she kept telling herself sternly. Her instinct that Mac was still in love with his ex-wife should be kept in mind, and the fact that she was here to help him win a contract.

Then the memory of his lips against hers seemed to close out all those other sensible thoughts.

'I do believe the men are going to join us,' Nancy said with a grin as she bustled out onto the patio with a bottle of champagne, which she put in an ice bucket by the table.

'You are going to a lot of trouble,' Melissa said, standing up to go over and join her. She wished Nancy would let her help. Several times she had been into the kitchen to offer assistance and each time she had been refused.

'There's not much to do for a barbecue.' Nancy reached over and lit the candles in the centre of the table, then went round to light the oil lamps at the side of the pool. 'There,' she said with pleasure, stepping back to observe her handiwork. 'Now all we need are the men. I thought I heard the door of the office open a few moments ago, so

with a bit of luck...' She trailed off as J.B. and Mac
stepped outside from the kitchen.

'At last,' she said. 'You know, J.B., Mac is here to have
a romantic weekend with his new fiancée, not to lock himself away in your office for hours on end. There will be
enough time for business tomorrow.'

J.B. looked at Melissa and then at Mac. 'You've got
engaged?'

'I decided I better keep tight hold of her, J.B.,' Mac said
with a smile. 'When you've got a good woman, you
shouldn't let her slip away.'

Mac glanced over at Melissa. She had changed into a
short white skirt and turquoise top after her swim. Her hair
was brought back in a ponytail, exposing the long, creamy
length of her neck. She looked about eighteen. How old
was she? he wondered, realising suddenly that he had
never asked. Come to think of it, there were a few things
he hadn't asked her.

The champagne exploded with a loud pop in the night
air as J.B. opened it and quickly poured the frothy liquid
into four long-stemmed glasses.

'Let's have a toast to your future,' he said, handing them
each a drink. 'May all of your troubles be little ones.'

Melissa's eyes held with Mac's over the rim of her
glass.

She wondered what he was thinking. He seemed to be
looking at her as if he had never seen her before. Maybe
he regretted kissing her. Maybe he had been kissing her
and thinking about his wife?

She didn't like that idea at all.

They took their seats at the table and Nancy served up
the food.

'You've got a lovely place here, Nancy,' Mac said.

'Yes, we like it. It goes cold in the winter, though. But
that has its compensations—we drive up to Mount
Charleston and do a bit of skiing.' Nancy reached across

and topped up Melissa's champagne. 'You and Melissa will have to come and join us this winter. It's great fun.'

'We'd enjoy that,' Mac replied nonchalantly.

Melissa looked across the table at him. By winter, Mac would probably be out of her life. What was it he had said earlier? 'We'll just have to bluff our way through it'…?

Well, he was certainly good at it.

He glanced over and smiled at her. He seemed perfectly at ease.

'So, have you got round to making any wedding plans yet?' Nancy asked, looking from one to the other of them, her eyes bright with interest.

'We're not really in any hurry.' Mac glanced again at Melissa. 'Are we, sweetheart?'

She felt her heart thump against her breast. 'No, not really,' she agreed quietly.

J.B. laughed. 'Well, if you change your mind, you are in no better city. You can get married here within twenty-four hours—get a licence at the courthouse, then a fifteen-minute service at one of the chapels, and the deed is done.'

'Yes, we could be your witnesses,' Nancy laughed. 'In fact, there's a drive-through wedding service at the other side of town. You don't even need to get out of the car,' she finished with a grin.

'That's a bit too fast for my liking,' Melissa said.

'I don't know,' Mac said with a grin, 'I kind of like the thought of that. No fuss. No need for all the agonising attention to small details. Sometimes when a wedding is too big the real meaning of it gets neglected under a *mélange* of who's sitting where and what colour the groom's mother and the bride's mother have chosen to wear.'

J.B. chuckled. 'That brings back memories, doesn't it, Nancy? I remember your mother and mine having a bit of a disagreement because they'd both chosen to wear yellow.'

'It was peach, as I recall,' Nancy corrected, then smiled.

'Our wedding did get a bit out of control, but I enjoyed the day itself. It was just the lead up to it that was stressful.' She glanced over at Melissa. 'If you want a big white wedding, though, you should hold out for it,' she said firmly. 'After all, it is supposed to be the most special day of your life.'

Melissa wished she hadn't started this. It wasn't as if she was really planning to marry Mac. 'We'll have to give it some more thought,' she said, trying to close the subject.

She wondered if Mac had been speaking from experience when he'd said a wedding could get of hand. She supposed he had. Probably his marriage to Kay had been a very big affair. Melissa remembered planning her wedding with Simon. They had started out with a small guest list and by the time her mother and his mother had finished it had suddenly increased to nearly one hundred people.

To her relief, the conversation turned to more general topics after that. They discussed Las Vegas. Nancy talked about her daughter. It was all very friendly and Melissa started to relax.

It was only as the time crept up towards midnight that tension started increasing inside her again—a feeling that escalated sharply when Nancy declared with a yawn, 'I suppose we should call it a night, let you two love birds turn in.'

Melissa's eyes brushed with Mac's and then she hurriedly looked away. 'I'll help you clear these things away, Nancy,' she said, standing up and helping the other woman as she started to remove the dishes.

When they returned from the kitchen, the men were still sitting at the table, deep in conversation about the new casino. 'Have a nightcap, Melissa?' J.B. offered as he poured some brandy out for himself and Mac.

'No, I'm going to turn in, J.B., but thanks all the same. See you in the morning.'

It was soothing to step from the patio into the air-conditioned balm of the bedroom. Melissa went to check on Lucy.

The little girl was fast asleep. She lay sprawled across the cot, the sheet tangled around the ends of her feet and Thomas the cat firmly held in her hand, her head resting on the knitted toy.

She straightened the sheet and stood looking down at her for a while before bending to give her a last goodnight kiss. Then she crept out of the room, leaving the door slightly ajar again.

Melissa paused, her eyes moving over the double bed. She remembered the way Mac had kissed her earlier and felt her heart starting to thud against her chest with hard, nervous strokes.

'We'll talk about this later,' he had said. What was there to talk about? Did he want to make sure that she realised he hadn't meant anything to be taken seriously?

She imagined him looking deep into her eyes and saying softly, Melissa, you were right, I am still in love with Kay. I should never have kissed you like that. This is a pretence, nothing more.

She took her night things from her overnight case and went into the bathroom. Of course, if she wanted this arrangement to be something more, she could always try to seduce him, she thought, turning on the shower and taking off her clothes.

She stepped under the forceful jet of water and held her face up to it in an attempt to clear her mind of such outrageous thoughts. The notion had crossed her mind a few times since agreeing to this weekend. But that was all it was, she asserted briskly. A fantasy.

She stepped out of the shower and dried herself before slipping into the long white nightdress and matching dressing gown.

The negligée had been an impulse buy, especially for this weekend. It wasn't at all revealing but it did skim her slender figure in a flattering way, emphasising her curves. When she had made the purchase, she had intended Mac to see her in it. She had told herself that if you wanted something you had to go after it. There was no point in playing the wallflower when the rose got all the attention.

But now, when it actually came to it, could she play the seductress? Melissa dried her hair and surveyed herself in the bathroom mirror. She had never been one for casual affairs. A one-night stand was not something she wanted to contemplate. But then, maybe it wouldn't be a one-night stand. Maybe she should take a chance, roll the dice and see what happened. She was in Nevada, after all!

She flicked off the light and returned to the bedroom.

It was a surprise to see Mac in the room. He had turned on one of the bedside lamps and was standing by the bed, unfastening the top buttons of his shirt.

He glanced over at her, and suddenly the nightdress felt like the most provocative thing she had ever worn. She felt his eyes moving over her as if he could see right through to her skin.

'Hi.' She smiled at him. 'I—I thought you would be a while longer.' She walked towards the bed, trying to pretend that this was a normal situation for her.

'And I thought we had unfinished business,' he said huskily.

She looked over at him, and her heart missed several beats. 'What do you mean?'

'You know what I mean…that kiss.'

'Oh, that!' She tried very hard to sound airily blasé as she reached to pull back the covers on the bed. Then she glanced at him from beneath her eyelashes. 'It was a very nice kiss.'

'Yes, very nice,' he murmured sardonically.

She sat on the bed, her back towards him, and pretended to be unfastening the ties of her dressing gown. 'But I suppose it didn't mean anything, did it?'

As soon as she had asked that question she wished she hadn't, because he made no reply, which she supposed in itself was an answer. She was right; it hadn't meant anything.

'It was a lovely evening.' She switched the subject abruptly, desperately trying to diminish the feeling of disappointment inside her.

'Apart from all that talk about weddings, you mean?' he asked nonchalantly.

She glanced over at him. 'I could have done without that,' she agreed tightly. 'I thought you went a bit overboard talking about what kind of wedding we should have. I felt embarrassed.'

'Yes, I noticed.' There was a hint of amusement in his low tone. 'You look very sexy when you are embarrassed, do you know that? Your eyes go a more intense shade of blue, and your skin gets a rosy glow across the top of your cheekbones.'

She frowned, the teasing note in his voice making her feel foolish. If he was aware that she had been embarrassed at dinner, did he realise just how nervous she was now? Did he know that she was falling in love with him?

The question came from out of nowhere and the shock of it stilled her heart to an alarming degree.

'Melissa?' His voice seemed to be coming from a great distance away.

'Yes, I heard you.' Her voice was sharper than she intended.

'Hey, it was only a bit of fun,' he said softly. 'I was only teasing.'

'I know.' She wanted him to go away, leave her alone. She needed to think about this new revelation. Was she in love with Mac Schofield? The answer came back a very clear yes. Why else was she sitting here on this bed trying to think of ways of getting him into it with her? It was totally out of character.

'I'm sorry if I didn't seem amused, but weddings aren't really a happy subject for me.' The words were a subterfuge. She couldn't allow Mac to know that she wished their little charade was for real...how humiliating!

Melissa heard him curse under his breath. Then, instead of going away as she wanted, he came around the bed to crouch down beside her.

'Melissa, I'm so sorry,' he said earnestly. 'I didn't think.'

The sympathy in his tone made her feel worse.

'It's OK, you weren't to know,' she mumbled.

'But I should have known. You told me that it was nearly a year since you broke things off with Simon. I should have realised all that talk about weddings would stir up very raw feelings for you.'

She looked over at him, her eyes moving slowly over the handsome contours of his face. No man had a right to be so good-looking, she thought warily. She loved everything about him—the way his eyes crinkled at the corners when he laughed, the square line of his jaw, the sensuous curve of his lips. 'It's really ironic,' she said shakily, speaking almost to herself. 'This time last year I was breaking my heart over Simon...and now—' She broke off and took a deep breath. She couldn't end that sentence the way she wanted to; she couldn't say, And now I realise that all Simon really hurt was my pride. That, in fact, he had done her a favour. Simon had never made her feel like this, as if she wanted to melt into him. Never had her heart leapt when he so much as caught her eye.

'And now?' he prompted her gently.

'And now...' She closed her eyes. 'And now I realise that I should stay away from serious involvement. Romantically speaking, I'm a disaster waiting to happen.'

Mac smiled and touched the side of her face. 'Come on, Melissa. You're a bit young to be saying that.'

'I'm twenty-eight years of age, Mac.' She opened her

eyes and looked at him. Twenty-eight and she had only just fallen in love for the first time.

'You look about eighteen,' he said, tucking a silky strand of her hair behind her ear. 'A very beautiful eighteen.'

'Don't go overboard,' she warned him shakily.

He frowned. His eyes moved to her lips. She felt herself moistening them. Felt the dull thud of her heart against her chest. She ached for him to kiss her.

'I meant it. I think you are very beautiful, Melissa.' His voice was husky and subdued.

'But you were going to apologise for kissing me tonight, weren't you?' She pulled herself together and met his eyes levelly. 'You were going to say, Sorry, Melissa, I didn't mean for that to happen.'

'Maybe I was. I seem to recall you telling me that I wasn't your type. You also told me that I wasn't to touch you.' There was a teasing gleam in his eyes for a moment, and she smiled wryly.

'Yes, I did,' she remembered.

'Bearing that in mind, maybe I should apologise for the kiss. The trouble is, I liked it,' he murmured huskily. He traced a gentle finger along the edge of her lips; the impact was sensuously intoxicating. Melissa felt herself shudder with raw need. 'But this is supposed to be a business trip...I promised you I'd sleep on the floor and I always keep my promises.'

She felt herself leaning forward. She wanted him to kiss her again. She wanted to say, To hell with promises!

His eyes moved over her face. 'But I want you, Melissa. I want you...badly.' His lips twisted in a wry smile. 'Badly is probably the best word to describe how I feel.' His gaze slipped lower to the ties on her nightdress. 'Because if I were any kind of gentleman I wouldn't be thinking like this.'

'Maybe I don't want you to act like a gentleman tonight.' She felt every thump of her heart painfully against her ribs.

She saw the surprise in his eyes as he looked up at her.

'I don't want to sleep in this bed on my own,' she admitted softly. She reached up and touched his face, then leaned closer, and kissed him.

Wow! She could play the seductress after all, she thought hazily. And it felt wonderful.

He allowed her to take the lead for a moment. Melissa was the one kissing him, her fingers lacing through the darkness of his hair, drawing him closer.

Her lips moved softly against his, shyly hesitant, yet enticing, impatient for him to return her kisses, sweetly giving herself, yet provocatively and brazenly tantalising.

When he took control and kissed her back, she felt a pleasure so fierce that it took her breath away.

He reached and unfastened the ties of her dressing gown. Her heart seemed to speed up in a wild and uneven rhythm as slowly, and very deliberately he sat back and started to undress her, first pushing down the dressing gown, then taking the delicate spaghetti straps of her nightdress and pushing them down as well. She felt her breasts harden as his fingers brushed against them, and the delicate satin material was pulled down with deliberate force.

She sat very still as he looked at her. 'You are so beautiful, Melissa,' he breathed huskily.

There was something overwhelming and erotic about the fact that she was in such a state of undress and he was fully clothed. He reached out to touch her and she inhaled sharply at the exquisite tremor of sensual excitement which immediately flared.

Melissa closed her eyes as his hand stroked over the naked curve of her breast. She could think of nothing except how wonderful it felt.

He moved closer, and his lips were hard and hungry

against hers, his hands stroking her breasts, teasing and tormenting her.

Melissa felt herself being brought backwards down against the bed. The soft cotton of his chinos and the silk of his shirt were pressed against her. They felt abrasive against the sensitised heat of her skin. She suddenly felt impatient to feel his skin against hers and she stroked her hands over his chest, found the buttons of his shirt and started to unfasten them.

He had a fabulous body, broad and strong. With each button that was undone she stroked her hands over the powerful contours of his chest, running her fingers through the dark whorls of hair before letting them stroke lower to the flat planes of his stomach, then lower still...

He smiled and then bent to kiss the side of her face. 'Be patient,' he whispered teasingly into her ear, nibbling at the sensitive skin and making her laugh.

While he was kissing her, his hands caught hold of the negligée and pulled it upwards. Suddenly she felt the full powerful force of him against her. The feeling was sensationally erotic; it brought red-hot heat coursing through her veins. Her laughter stopped as his lips covered her mouth, tasting her, possessing her with a dominance that brought her fully under his control.

She arched her back, moaning feverishly as his lips moved to kiss her breasts, first one rosy nipple then the other, circling his tongue over her heated flesh and making her quiver with urgent, sweet need.

His hand smoothed over the slender lines of her body and stroked her hips, her thighs, without touching the core of her need. She wanted him so much, and she told him so ardently as he made no attempt to assuage that need.

He kissed her lips again, his thumbs rasping over the taut lines of her nipples.

'I've been wanting to do this since the first moment I set eyes on this delectable body at close quarters,' he told her huskily. 'Those little tops…that you barely wear around the garden… I've longed to get hold of them…and pull them up…or off…or both…' The words were punctuated by little kisses.

Then suddenly he pulled away from her and stood up. She sat up, pushing her hair out of her eyes, frowning. She needed him; he wasn't going to stop, was he? Melissa hardly had time to register the fact that he was ridding himself of the rest of his clothes before he was back beside her.

'That's better,' he murmured, bringing her close in against the naked length of him. 'Now, where were we, hmm?' he murmured teasingly.

'I don't know.' She wound her arms up and around his neck, her eyes meeting his playfully. 'Where were we?'

'Somewhere around about here?' He moved, and feverish gasps shivered through her as he took the ultimate possession of her body. She couldn't answer him, couldn't think about anything except the little shudders of pleasure which darted through her. The feeling was exquisite, hedonistic paradise. He moved slowly against her at first, then his lovemaking became unbridled, fierce, demanding. She gave herself up to it with total abandonment, revelling in the power he had over her senses, totally oblivious to everything except the delights and the appeasement of the wild hunger inside her.

She clung to him as the world seemed to explode around her, leaving her dazed, breathless, and, suddenly, incredibly sleepy.

He cradled her in his arms and kissed her tenderly. She wanted to tell him that she loved him; the words wavered precariously on the edge of her lips. Closing her eyes, she snuggled closer in against his chest as he brought the covers around them. Then she drifted into sleep.

CHAPTER TEN

MELISSA woke up feeling disorientated. The sun had risen. Pearly pink light shimmered over the room.

She stretched luxuriously in the large bed, her hand reaching out into the empty space next to her. And suddenly memories of the night before returned with full force, and she turned her head to look at the pillow beside hers. She was alone.

Melissa remembered the way Mac had kissed her last night, remembered the explosive compelling passion that it had ignited. Remembered the touch of his hard body against hers. Then she recollected that she had openly invited him into her bed, and the dreamy revelry gave way to reproach. What would Mac think of her this morning?

She sat up, holding the sheets over her naked body, her eyes searching the room for him, but she was quite alone.

Leaning her head back against the pillows, she allowed her mind to drift back over the previous night, searching through each moment of it.

She was trying to remember if she had told him she loved him; she felt almost sure she had. He had spoken only words of desire to her; she had no difficulty recalling that. How was she going to face him today? She felt such a fool. And yet she couldn't honestly say that she regretted sleeping with him. It had been the most incredible night. Never had she felt so sensually alive. Mac had aroused her and taken her to the heights of ecstasy with such ease, such tenderness, that just thinking about it brought a vivid resurgence of desire from out of nowhere.

So she wouldn't think about it, she told herself sternly. It would be best to just draw a veil over last night, forget it happened. Quickly she got up and reached for her dressing gown, then walked over to the nursery. Lucy's cot was empty.

Melissa glanced at the clock on the wall and was dismayed to see that it was nearly nine a.m. She couldn't believe that she had slept so long.

Hurriedly she turned and went into the bathroom to shower and change.

She dressed in a primrose-yellow sundress and paid careful attention to her hair and make-up. She wanted to look cool and composed when she saw Mac. She didn't want him to know how vulnerable and uncertain she felt about what had happened between them. As an added shield, she put on a pair of dark sunglasses, then stepped out of the bedroom onto the patio. She had intended to walk round to the kitchen from outside but, in fact, she found Mac and Nancy sitting at the table on the patio, Lucy between them in a high chair.

The heat of the morning was intense, the sky a clear, deep blue. The three of them were under the shade of an enormous striped awning that was pulled down from the side of the house. Mac was drinking iced tea, his chair facing towards her.

'Here she is now,' he said as he looked up and saw her approach.

She felt her heart lurch crazily as he got up from his chair politely and smiled at her.

He looked bronzed and incredibly handsome in a cream shirt and pale chinos. He also seemed very relaxed and at ease as he reached to kiss her on the cheek.

His closeness, the tang of his aftershave brought back vivid memories of what they had shared last night. The recollection of his body pressing down against hers, of his hands on her breasts, his lips heated and fervent on hers, arose very forcibly in her mind.

'Good morning, sweetheart,' he murmured huskily as he drew away and looked down at her.

She had never been more grateful for a pair of sunglasses in all her life. 'Morning.' She managed a smile and took the chair he pulled out for her.

'Good morning, Nancy,' she said, looking across at the other woman, thankful for her presence.

'How did you sleep?' Nancy asked, reaching to pour her a glass of the iced tea.

'Just fine, thank you.' She looked across at Lucy who was eating a piece of toast, her little fingers buttery and sticky. She gave Melissa a winning smile.

'What time did you get up, Mac? I didn't hear you.' She was very pleased at how light her voice sounded: she was handling this OK, she told herself soothingly.

'Around about seven-thirty. Lucy started to sing to herself and I thought I'd better get her up before she woke you. You were dead to the world,' he added with a grin.

'Must have been the champagne,' she replied, sipping her ice-cold drink and centring her attention on Lucy. Maybe she shouldn't have said that, she thought. She hadn't even been in the slightest bit tipsy last night. Then she shrugged to herself. What the hell? Maybe she could blame the whole of her outrageous behaviour last night on the champagne and it would get her off the emotional hook she felt she had snared herself on. She hoped to high heaven she hadn't told Mac she loved him. It would be too humiliating in the extreme.

The phone rang in the house and Nancy got up from the table. 'Won't be a moment.'

Melissa watched her go with a feeling of trepidation. She wasn't ready to be left alone with Mac just yet.

'How are you this morning?' he asked in a low tone.

'I'm fine.' She couldn't look at him. Instead she tried to concentrate on Lucy.

'Fine as in wonderful, or fine as in just don't ask?' Mac continued gently.

She hesitated, the direct question making her uncomfortable. 'I don't know,' she answered honestly. 'I—I was out of control last night. It's not something I'm used to.'

His lips curved in wry amusement. 'You aren't trying to tell me it was the champagne?'

'I don't know. Maybe it was.'

He reached across and took off the sunglasses she wore. The gesture made her flinch away from him. She felt as if her shield was down, her defences crumbling.

'I've got news for you, honey. We were both stone-cold sober,' he said decisively.

'Were we?' She felt totally out of her depth.

His eyes raked over her heated countenance. Her eyes looked enormous in her small face. He saw the shadows of consternation in them, the vulnerable unease.

'You know we were,' he said gently.

She didn't have a chance to answer, because Nancy came bustling back to the table. 'Sorry about that,' she said brightly, retaking her seat. 'That was Simon Wesley, Melissa. He's in town for the meeting this afternoon. Said he might pop over to see you later. I told him not to make it too late because you and Mac were going out to dinner.'

Melissa had forgotten that Nancy had offered to babysit for them tonight. She wondered if Mac really wanted to take her out to dinner. It was one thing him asking, quite another Nancy pushing him into it.

She looked across at him. He said nothing.

'By the way, Mac, the table's booked for seven-thirty,' Nancy said. 'So don't let J.B. detain you today.'

'I won't, Nancy,' he replied easily. He finished his drink. 'On that note, I suppose I'd better get going.'

'J.B. left earlier,' Nancy explained to Melissa. 'Mac's taking his convertible and meeting him in town.'

Mac bent and kissed Lucy. 'Bye, angel, you be good

for Melissa,' he said softly. Then he looked over at Melissa. 'Walk with me to the car?' he said softly. 'So I can say goodbye properly?'

Melissa was startled by the request and it must have shown in her face.

Nancy laughed. 'I wish J.B. was this romantic. I get a peck on the cheek if I'm lucky.'

Melissa smiled, put her sunglasses back on and slowly got to her feet.

As soon as they were out of earshot of Nancy, Mac said, 'I just want to check with you that you'll be able to manage Lucy?'

'Of course I will.' Melissa frowned, aware that she was more than a little disappointed that this was his reason for wanting to get her on her own. 'Don't you trust me?'

'If I didn't trust you I wouldn't have asked you to take care of her,' he told her firmly. 'No, I just want to make sure that you feel OK about having her for the day. You'll find all her things in the bag by her buggy. She usually has her lunch at about twelve-thirty, and sometimes she has a sleep afterwards—'

'Mac, will you stop worrying? I'm perfectly capable of taking care of Lucy.'

They stopped by J.B.'s white convertible. 'I've written the number of my mobile down by Nancy's phone in the hall. Take it and put it in your purse. Then, if you have any problems, ring me immediately.'

'OK. Lunch twelve-thirty, sleep in the afternoon, ring you if there's a problem.' She relayed his words parrot-fashion. 'Got it. Now go, and don't worry.'

He grinned and tipped up her chin with a light finger. 'And I'll see you for dinner this evening.'

Just the lightest touch of his hand sent her pulse soaring. 'Well, I suppose it will please Nancy,' she said flippantly. She wouldn't admit for one moment that it would please her, that she would count the hours until tonight.

'He reached and took off her sunglasses. 'I don't like these things,' he said impatiently. 'I can't tell what you are really thinking when you wear them.'

'I'm thinking it's hot and it's bright and I can't see without them,' she said, trying to get them back from him.

He held them out of her reach. 'I'll look forward to tonight.' He lowered his voice to a deep, sexy tone that made her wonder if he was referring to dinner or to later than that. The thought that once again she would be sharing a room with him made her skin go hot, made the blood pump through her body as if it were oil-fired.

He watched her for a moment without saying anything. Then he bent down and his lips met hers in a swift yet piercingly sweet kiss. 'See you later.'

He handed her back the sunglasses. She couldn't find her voice to make an answer.

Mac climbed into the car and started the engine.

'Oh, and by the way,' he said as he slipped it into gear and took off the handbrake, 'be careful around Simon Wesley.'

'What do you mean?' She gathered her thoughts with difficulty.

'You know what I mean. We both know that the guy has got more than a passing interest in you, and, as your part-time fiancé, I'd rather you kept your distance.'

Then, with a wave of his hand, he was pulling away from her down the driveway, a haze of dust hanging in the air behind the vehicle, obscuring it from view.

She could have done without the reminder that she was just part-time in his life. Coming on the heels of his kiss, it confused her. Was his objection to Simon because he was jealous in any way, or was he just thinking about their charade?

Slowly she made her way back round the side of the house.

The day with Nancy and Lucy seemed to fly by. After

breakfast they went into town and did some shopping. Melissa bought herself a new dress for her dinner with Mac. It was very glamorous, a black, beaded creation. Sexy yet elegantly discreet. A total spur-of-the-moment impulse, egged on by Nancy who thought she looked gorgeous in it.

Afterwards they had lunch, and then headed back to the ranch. Lucy fell asleep in the back of the car, so Melissa put her down in the cot when they got back.

About to tuck Thomas the cat in next to her, Melissa noticed that its tail was practically off now, its stitching very much in need of sorting out. She took the toy with her as she returned outside.

'Have you got a needle and thread, Nancy?' she asked.

'Yes, I've got a sewing box inside. I'll get it for you.'

The two women sat under the shade of the awning, talking as Melissa worked on repairing the toy. The heat was intense, too fierce to sit out in for very long.

There was a sleepy, relaxed atmosphere. Melissa finished her work and felt like lying down for a nap herself.

The sound of a car pulling around by the front of the house disturbed the tranquillity of the afternoon.

'That might be Simon,' Nancy said, getting up to investigate.

Sure enough, a few moments later she reappeared around the side of the house, Simon in tow.

He was wearing a pair of shorts and a blue shirt, and he looked very much at ease chatting to Nancy, his arm tucked through hers.

'Hi, Melissa.' He sat on the swing chair opposite. 'Whew, it's hot, isn't it? Must be at least a hundred and ten, and that's in the shade.'

'How about if I fix us all a frozen margarita?' Nancy said.

'Sounds excellent; thanks, Nancy.' Simon leaned back

in the chair and looked over at Melissa as they were left alone. 'You didn't ring me,' he accused softly.

'I haven't had a chance; I'm sorry, Simon. Things have been a bit hectic since I saw you last.'

Her eyes moved over him for a moment. It seemed incredible that she had once imagined he'd broken her heart. She felt nothing now looking into his eyes, nothing except a mild feeling of relief that they hadn't actually gone through with those wedding plans.

'I'll forgive you, because I heard you had other things on your mind. I bumped into Mac this afternoon at the meeting for the casino. He told me you'd got engaged.' He hesitated for a moment before adding, 'I wish you every happiness, Melissa.'

'Thanks.' Melissa tried to look at ease with his congratulations. She was a bit surprised that Mac had volunteered that information.

'He's a lucky guy,' Simon said quietly. 'I told him so, in no uncertain terms.'

'Did you?'

'You know I'll always regret losing you, don't you?'

'Simon, I don't want to talk about the past.'

'I know, but I just want to tell you: I still have feelings for you.'

Melissa started to say something and he cut across her. 'I know you are engaged to someone else now, but I just wanted you to know how I feel. Just in case you might be on the rebound.'

'Rebound?' Melissa looked at him, genuinely bewildered by the statement.

'From me.'

'Oh!' Melissa had to swallow down a nervous urge to giggle. 'No...no, Simon, I'm not on the rebound.'

'I see.' He looked disappointed for a moment. 'OK. But we are still friends, right?'

'I don't see why not,' Melissa agreed.

'And my offer of a job still stands.'

'Were you serious?'

'Certainly was. Now that I've got the contract for this new casino, I need all the expertise I can lay my hands on. It's quite an exciting challenge as well. They want me to re-create a rainforest in the centre of the casino.'

'That does sound interesting,' Melissa agreed.

'So what do you say?'

'I don't know, Simon; I'll have to give it some thought. What will it entail?'

'*Very* good remuneration for a start. You'd have to move out here to Nevada while we set it up, get a good team around us. The company will pay for all that, obviously.'

Melissa shook her head. The job sounded very exciting, but moving to Nevada...she wasn't sure about that at all. 'It sounds wonderful, but I don't want to move—plus I've got Mac to consider,' she added, mindful of the fact that she was supposed to be engaged.

'Don't give me an answer just now,' Simon told her decisively. 'Have lunch with me next week when you're back in L.A. and we'll talk about it.'

'I don't know about lunch, Simon,' she said quickly.

'Look, no strings, no ulterior motives. I'm really sincere about the job.'

Melissa nodded. 'OK, I'll do some thinking.'

The fierce heat of the desert sun had gone down in a blaze of orange as Mac pulled the car up in front of the ranch. He walked around the side of the house, glad to be back. He was looking forward to the evening with Melissa. In truth, the anticipation of it had been like a shining beacon: it had kept him going through a gruelling and intense meeting.

He noticed Lucy's toy cat sitting on the swing chair and went to pick it up on his way past. He glanced at it idly as he walked towards the kitchen door, then frowned as he noticed that someone had patched it up. They'd taken a lot of trouble and done a very good job as well.

'Oh, hi, Mac.' Nancy turned with a smile as he came in. 'Had a good day?'

'Yeah, not bad, thanks, Nancy.' He held up the toy. 'Did you do this?'

Nancy laughed. 'No. That was Melissa. We've had a wonderful day together.'

'Lucy was good, then?' Mac murmured. He was staring down at the toy, wondering why its restored appearance should disturb him so much.

'She was an angel. And Melissa is so good with her— that little girl really adores her. It warms your heart to see them together; it really does.'

'Does it?' Mac felt a sudden cold surge of something akin to fear.

'Would you like a drink?' Nancy went to put the kettle on.

'No, thanks.' He stood where he was for a moment, trying to clarify his thoughts.

'Simon popped over this afternoon; I think he wants Melissa to work with him on the garden design for the casino,' Nancy continued. 'It would be fun if you both ended up working on the same project, wouldn't it?'

'Yes…fun.' Mac remembered his encounter with Simon Wesley earlier. Something had impelled him to tell the guy that he'd just got engaged to Melissa. In retrospect, he had probably gone over the top. He'd told him he was head over heels in love, had never felt like this about anyone before.

Simon had just looked at him. 'I'm glad you're happy,' he'd murmured. 'Of course, it's exactly a year this weekend since we should have been married. Coincidence, that…isn't it?' Then he'd walked away, as calm as could be.

Mac moved away from the doorway. 'Excuse me, Nancy; I'll just go and see how Melissa is doing.'

Mac could hear Lucy's laughter as he walked down the corridor. Their bedroom was empty, the door to the *en-suite* bathroom ajar. Through it, Mac could see Melissa kneeling by the bath, bathing Lucy.

He stopped in the doorway and watched without either of them being aware of his presence.

'Here comes the plane one more time,' Melissa said, smiling as she swept the sponge over Lucy and let the water trickle over her.

Lucy chuckled heartily. The sound was infectious, and jolly. To a casual onlooker the scene was the quintessence of harmony, mother and child enjoying themselves. Except Melissa wasn't Lucy's mother. She wasn't really even his girlfriend; she'd just been playing a part. A part that maybe they had both got carried away with. Especially Melissa. She'd been upset last night...all that talk about weddings and on the very eve of what should have been her wedding anniversary to Simon. The cold feeling tightened in Mac's chest.

What was it Nancy had said? 'That little girl really adores her.'

He couldn't allow Lucy to get emotionally attached to Melissa. Hell, he had felt as if the stuffing had been knocked out of him when Kay had walked away, but it would have been much worse had Lucy been older, been emotionally attached to her.

And if Lucy's mother could walk away without a backward glance, couldn't any woman? Especially a woman who was still hung up on her old boyfriend. He had to safeguard Lucy against that kind of hurt, at all costs.

'More, Issa,' she squealed when Melissa stopped the game.

Lucy's laughter turned to a squeal of delight as Mac stepped into the room and she caught sight of him.

'Dadda,' she shouted, trying to get up out of the water.

Melissa turned, and her eyes met his. 'Hi.' She smiled. 'How long have you been there?'

'Long enough. I didn't like to disturb you, you were doing such a good job.'

Melissa lifted Lucy out of the water and wrapped her in a warm, fluffy towel, rubbing her briskly. 'We're just about finished anyway.'

Mac went across. 'Here, let me.' He lifted the child up, swinging her high. 'How is Daddy's little girl?'

He kissed her and looked across at Melissa. 'I take it she's been good?'

'Yes, no trouble at all.' Melissa stood up and wished she'd had a chance to tidy her appearance before he'd got here. She was acutely conscious of the fact that there were wet splotches of bath water on her pale yellow dress and her hair was hanging in damp tendrils from where Lucy had splashed her. She turned away from him, busying herself picking up Lucy's clothes from the floor. 'What sort of a day have you had?' she asked brightly.

'It's been OK. All the better for getting back here.'

She looked over at him briefly; he was smiling at Lucy. 'Do you still want to go for this meal tonight, or are you too tired?'

'Of course I want to go out.' He transferred Lucy to his other side so he could look over at Melissa more clearly. 'The least I can do is take you out for a meal.'

Melissa frowned. Why did that sound so formal, as if she were the babysitter or something?

'Why don't you go and get ready? I'll finish off here with Lucy.'

'I was just going to give her a bottle—'

'I know, but I'll do it.' Mac walked across and took the clothes from her hands. 'You've done enough. Hasn't she, Lucy?' he asked the child playfully. 'Come on, kiss Melissa goodnight, and Daddy will give you your milk.'

Lucy leaned forward with a sweet smile and kissed Melissa on the cheek. For a moment she was drawn close against them both, enveloped in the baby's warmth, then Mac was moving away from her.

CHAPTER ELEVEN

'It was really kind of Nancy and J.B. to offer to babysit, wasn't it?' Melissa broke the silence between them in the car.

'Yes, they are a nice couple. I hope Lucy behaves for them. I'd have felt better if she'd fallen asleep before we left. She seemed a bit fractious.'

'That might have been my fault. She slept for over an hour this afternoon.'

'She usually does that.' He glanced sideways at her. 'You were great with her today. Thank you.'

'You don't have to thank me,' she said huskily. 'I enjoyed myself.' Melissa wondered if this awkward, strained feeling between them was in her imagination. Mac seemed cool somehow. It was hard to imagine that this was the same man who had made such passionate love to her last night.

The lights of Vegas shimmered invitingly out of the darkness of the night. Enticements to try your luck, invitations to visit wedding chapels and gaming tables, restaurants, bars and shows bombarded them in swirling, colourful cascades of illumination.

Mac pulled into a car park and they walked through one of the casinos towards the lifts that would take them up to the restaurant.

The building was extremely opulent: designer shops along marble and gold halls; massive gaming areas lit by the sparkle of chandeliers. Melissa noticed the cars on top of some of the gambling machines: Mustangs and Mercedes, vying for attention, waiting to be won. 'We'll have a flutter later,' Mac said as she paused to look at them.

'Are you feeling lucky?' she asked, a teasing light in her eyes as she looked up at him.

His eyes moved over her. She looked sensational in the black dress. It skimmed her figure in a sensually provocative way, emphasising her curves, the tiny beaded straps criss-crossing over the softly tanned skin at her shoulders and her back. He wanted to say, I was, until I ran into Simon Wesley this afternoon. Until I stopped and scrutinised this situation.

He smiled. 'Well, I certainly got lucky last night, didn't I?'

Melissa didn't like those words. She wanted him to take them back. They made her feel cheap.

'Come on, let's get away from these crowds.' He put an arm lightly around her waist. She walked beside him, her mind racing. Was she imagining this coolness? Was she being over-sensitive because she felt vulnerably unsure of him?

The restaurant had fabulous views out over the strip. It was a romantic setting, with subdued candlelight, and private booths.

Mac ordered a bottle of wine and they scanned the menus for a while.

Or, at least, Melissa pretended to study the menu—her eyes kept darting across the table towards him.

He was wearing a dark suit which made him look sensually magnetic. She had noticed, as they walked through the casino, that a lot of women sent admiring glances in his direction, yet he seemed unaware of the power of his looks, the effect of his smile.

'So Lucy wasn't a problem today?'

'She was wonderful,' Melissa assured him. 'And if you thank me for looking after her again I'm going to fall out with you.'

He gave a lopsided grin—a rueful, attractive look. 'I don't want that to happen, but I do have a lot to thank you for,' he asserted firmly. 'Thanks to you, I've got a permanent contract with J.B.'

'You've definitely got the contract?' Melissa's eyes widened.

He nodded. 'J.B. told me today. The other good news is that I'm going to be heading the team on this new casino.'

'Mac, that's marvellous. Congratulations.'

He grinned. 'As I said, I couldn't have done it without your help.'

'I think you would have done it anyway,' Melissa maintained. 'J.B. wouldn't employ you if you weren't the best man for the job.'

'Maybe.' He shrugged. 'But I appreciate your help in the matter.' He raised his glass. 'So here's to you. As J.B. is fond of saying, behind every successful man is a good woman.'

She lifted her glass and touched it against his. 'Well done,' she said gently.

Mac looked across the candlelight and met her eyes, a sudden seriousness stealing over his expression.

'So, you're off the hook now,' he said suddenly.

'Off the hook?'

'Our phoney engagement,' he enlightened her. 'You won't have to play your part for very much longer.'

She felt her heart speeding up, hitting against her chest in hard, heavy strokes. 'Well, that's a relief.' Never had a smile been so hard to find. 'I don't think I was much of an actress.'

'On the contrary, I think you played the part pretty well.' His eyes held hers steadily across the table. 'Even had me fooled for a while.'

She swallowed hard, trying to compose her thoughts. Was he giving her the elbow? Her task was finished and so was she? After last night, and the heat of their passion, it was hard to believe. But it really sounded like it.

'So, where do we go from here?' he asked quietly.

'Home, on J.B.'s private jet?' She tried to cover her uncertainty by sounding frivolous.

'You know what I mean.' He was unwavering. 'I'm talking about us, about what happened between us last night.'

She felt her skin prickle with heat as his eyes raked over her, deeply probing and intense. 'I know you are,' she said quietly. 'I'm sorry; I just feel a bit unsure about last night.'

The waitress arrived to take their orders. Food suddenly felt like a mundane problem to be dispensed with quickly. Yet when they were left alone neither of them broached the subject again readily.

'Do you regret sleeping with me?' Mac asked quietly, after a moment of tense silence.

'Don't you think that I should be asking you that question?' Her heart thudded unevenly against her chest. 'You asked me to accompany you here for business reasons. I suppose last night is a complication you could do without.'

'I wouldn't go that far,' he said with a gleam of amusement. His eyes raked over her, and he lowered his voice. 'I wanted you, Melissa; you know I did.'

She felt herself melt inside.

'Last night was a mutual flare of attraction. We're both adults—we know it happens,' he said softly.

Melissa didn't like his analysis. For her, it had been more than a flare of attraction, but she couldn't tell him that. She felt that as well as giving her body to him last night she had bared her soul. She needed to keep part of herself back now, so that her pride could evaluate the situation.

'I suppose you're right.' She took a deep breath. 'Just as long as you don't think I'm in the habit of having casual affairs.'

'I don't think that at all,' he said quietly. Then he smiled. 'And that goes for me, too.'

She couldn't return his smile, couldn't heal the hurt she felt inside at his words, even though she knew she had no right to feel hurt. They had enjoyed a night of passion. She couldn't, and shouldn't, expect him to declare his undying love. It just wasn't realistic.

If she thought about the situation positively, she supposed she should feel relieved that he hadn't guessed how deeply her emotions were involved.

'I'd like for us to continue seeing each other when we get back to L.A.,' he murmured suddenly.

'Well, I have to finish your garden, don't I?' She couldn't hold back the flippant reply. 'So of course we will see each other.'

He frowned.

She sighed, 'I'm sorry, Mac. That didn't come out the way it should. I suppose what I'm saying is that I don't want to be just a notch on your bedpost. I've been through a relationship like that with Simon. I want someone who thinks I'm special, someone who really cares about me. Someone who will restore my faith in men and be there for me.'

'That's quite a list.' His lips twisted ruefully.

'Just call me an old romantic.' She took a deep breath. 'I've been hurt once by a man. I don't want to go down that path again...'

'You're not over him, are you?'

She looked away from him. She was well over Simon, but she wasn't going to open up and tell him that. Not yet. Not until she knew whether or not he wanted to even try at a relationship with her.

'Nancy mentioned that he had called by today.'

'He wanted to tell me that his job offer was still open.'

'I've got a feeling that's not the only thing on offer where Simon is concerned—'

'Oh, come on, Mac! He talked about a job, that's it.'

'No, he didn't. He told you he missed you and that you're probably on the rebound with me.'

Mac watched the colour suffuse her face. 'Right on target, aren't I?'

'It doesn't matter what he said,' Melissa said quietly. 'The truth is that I couldn't get emotionally involved with Simon again. He hurt me too much, and I'm not about to go back for a second helping.'

'Doesn't stop you loving someone, though...does it?' There was a poignant ring to those words. Melissa wondered suddenly if he was reflecting on his own feelings for his ex-wife.

She studied his face across the table—the dark eyes were piercingly intent, yet there was no hint of any emotion.

The ring of his mobile phone interrupted them.

'Sorry,' he said, reaching to take it out of his jacket pocket.

She watched as he answered the call. Saw his expression change.

'No, it's OK, Nancy, you've done the right thing,' he said. 'Yes...we'll be right back.'

'What's wrong?' Melissa asked anxiously as he hung up.

'Lucy's fretful.' Mac put his hand up to attract the waitress's attention. 'She's got a temperature and she's crying—I could hear her in the background. I'm really sorry about this, Melissa, but we're going to have to go back.'

The bill was paid and, minutes later, they were making their way back down through the casino. Melissa could hardly keep up with Mac's long strides.

'I'm sure it can't be anything too serious,' she tried to reassure him as they reached the car. 'She was fine this afternoon.'

'Yeah, I know, I keep telling myself that.' He opened

the passenger door for her and then went round to the other side. 'But Nancy isn't the type to panic unnecessarily. She's a mother herself.'

Melissa felt a dart of trepidation. He was right; Nancy wasn't the type to spook easily.

'When I think about it, she's been getting a temperature off and on a lot recently. When I mentioned it to my doctor, he put it down to teething. Now I wonder.'

Soon, the lights of the strip were left behind and they were on the empty desert roads. Neither of them spoke. Melissa watched the car headlights slice through the night and tried not to panic.

There couldn't be that much wrong with Lucy, she kept telling herself. She would have seen some sign of it today, or at least tonight when she had bathed her.

Mac didn't so much park the car outside the front of the ranch as abandon it. Then they both raced in to be met by Nancy. She looked completely distraught.

'I rang my friend, Ryan. He's a doctor, and he said he'd come over and take a look at her.'

'Did you describe her symptoms over the phone?' Mac asked, hurrying past her towards the nursery.

'Yes...'

Nancy's voice faltered and broke. Melissa could see the fear in her eyes and her heart seemed to falter and stop beating altogether for the next few moments.

'What did he say?' She wondered if her voice was as loud as it sounded in her ears. She didn't remember ever being this scared.

'He said it sounded like meningitis.'

Afterwards, Melissa would always wonder how they got through those next few hours. It all seemed like some kind of bad dream. She kept going back over the day in her mind, looking for signs that she now imagined she must have missed. Guilt and fear mingled inside her, churning her up. If she had realised that Lucy was ill, maybe this could have been prevented, maybe vital treatment given earlier.

Outwardly Mac remained composed, even after Nancy's doctor had told them that they should get Lucy to the hospital. Mac was calm and in control, holding Lucy and soothing her softly.

Her crying seemed easier now that her father held her, his quiet reassurance perhaps taking some of the terror away from her.

Melissa didn't ask if she could accompany them to the hospital; she just went. J.B. drove them there. It was a nightmare journey, and one Melissa would remember for a very long time.

J.B. dropped them at the emergency room and went to park the car, while Melissa hurried inside with Mac.

There followed several hours of uncertainty. Doctors came and went. Tests were ordered. Mac filled in forms and talked to medical staff. A nurse asked Melissa if she was the child's mother. She shook her head and they asked her to wait outside.

Mac didn't look round as she left. He had other things on his mind. She found J.B. sitting in the corridor on one of those stiff plastic chairs that were totally uncomfortable. 'Any news?' He jumped up immediately.

She shook her head. 'They're running more tests.'

They sat side by side for a while, neither talking, neither wanting to voice their fears.

When Mac joined them a little while later, they both looked up at him with hopeful eyes.

'They don't know if it is meningitis. They're sending for another doctor. She seems stable now, at any rate.'

'Well, that's something,' J.B. said heavily.

'Yeah.' Mac raked a hand wearily through the thick darkness of his hair. Melissa longed to go and put her arms around him, comfort him.

'Look, I don't suppose there's any point in us all staying here,' Mac continued. 'You get back to Nancy; I'll ring as soon as there is any news.'

J.B. hesitated. 'You go, J.B.,' Melissa said gently. 'I'll stay with Mac.'

He nodded. 'OK. I suppose Nancy will be starting to fret. I'll go and update her. But you be sure to ring when there is some news.'

Mac nodded. 'I will. And thanks, J.B.'

After he had gone, a nurse came out and told them to sit in one of the waiting rooms. She opened a door through to some more comfortable seats, then asked if they would like coffee.

They both declined the offer.

Melissa sat next to Mac. His face was grey, his eyes far-away.

She searched for something to say, something to make him feel better. Then she reached to take hold of his hand.

He glanced at her—he seemed almost dazed.

'She's in good hands, Mac,' Melissa whispered confidently.

'Yes, I guess so.'

She squeezed his hand and didn't let go of him.

'It's just that she looks so tiny and helpless,' he said, his voice strained. 'If only I could change places with her, if it could be me in there instead of her.'

'She'll pull through,' Melissa said positively. 'She's a strong little girl, full of determination.' Even as she was saying the words, she was praying that they were true.

'She's never been ill before,' he said. 'Not really ill, not more than a cold or teething.' He shook his head. 'This is the worst feeling in the world. I've never felt so damn helpless in all my life.'

'It will be OK,' Melissa repeated determinedly. 'Children get ill, they get all sorts of things, but they're stronger than they look.'

'I hope you're right,' he grated, taking his hand away from hers. 'Do you think I should ring Kay?' he said suddenly. 'I mean, she is Lucy's mother—she has a right to know.'

'If you feel that you should, then do,' Melissa said softly.

He raked his hands through his hair. 'I don't know. She's never been interested before—'

A doctor came through the door and asked Mac if he could speak to him for a few minutes.

Melissa watched as Mac followed him out into the corridor. She could see them through the glass windows and she tried to scrutinise the expressions on Mac's face to discern what the doctor might be saying to him.

Mac looked up and their eyes met through the glass. For the first time he noticed the shadows in her violet-blue eyes, the extreme pallor of her skin. Her hands were tightly clenched on her knee. He reached and opened the door between them.

'Is it all right if Melissa comes in with me?' he asked the doctor quietly. 'She's the closest that Lucy has to a mother right now.'

The doctor nodded.

'They are ruling out meningitis,' Mac told her as she joined him. 'Her temperature is returning to normal—they think she has a viral infection.'

He put an arm round her as they followed the doctor into the small private room.

Lucy was asleep. Her little face was flushed, her blonde curls damp. She looked so tiny, so helpless.

'As I said, Mr Schofield, we believe she is over the worst now. We'll monitor her closely over the next few hours, but she seems to be OK.'

Melissa looked down at the child and felt like crying with relief.

'Why don't you both go home and get some sleep?' the

doctor suggested. 'We'll ring you if there is any change.' He turned away to talk to one of the nurses.

'I don't want to leave her,' Mac said quietly. Then he looked over at her. 'But you go, Melissa; you must be exhausted. It's nearly five in the morning.'

'Really?' Melissa shook her head. Then she let her breath out in a sigh. 'I don't feel in the slightest bit tired.' Her eyes moved back to Lucy. She was peaceful, her breathing even.

Mac's attention shifted from his baby to Melissa, allowing himself to shut everything out of his mind for a moment as he observed her. He saw the sweet tenderness in her expression as she watched Lucy.

Mac tightened the arm he held around her, squeezing her against his side. She looked up at him, startled out of her reverie.

Then he bent and kissed her lightly on the lips.

'Have I told you how special you are?' he whispered softly.

She leaned against him, drawing strength from his closeness, feeling herself relaxing against him.

For a while they stood there just looking down at Lucy, soothed by the quietness of her, by the soft, healthy colour that had returned to her cheeks.

'Like the quiet after the storm,' one of the nurses remarked, coming to check up on the baby and write something on one of the charts. 'Children can be such a worry, can't they?' She smiled at them both. 'I remember when my little boy got a concussion after a bad fall. You'd think, as a nurse, I would be perfectly calm.' She shook her head in a derogatory fashion. 'I would have gone completely to pieces if it hadn't been for my partner.' She put the chart back on the cot. 'Why don't you two go and have a coffee...relax? We'll take good care of Lucy and ring you as soon as she wakes up.'

Melissa thought that Mac was going to refuse the offer

but, to her surprise, he nodded. 'You've got my mobile number?'

'In large print,' the woman assured him with a smile as she hurried away.

Mac reached into the cot to touch the sleeping baby with a loving caress. 'We won't be long, Lucy,' he breathed.

Mac phoned Nancy and J.B. as they walked back out into the corridor. 'Lucy is out of danger,' he said, and Melissa could hear the deep relief in his voice as he uttered those words. 'We're going to get some breakfast in town,' Mac told Nancy. 'You get some sleep—the hospital has my number if there is any problem. And thank you, Nancy.'

'I'm not hungry, Mac,' Melissa protested as he led her outside. It was still dark, yet the heat of the night was intense. 'And maybe we shouldn't leave just yet.'

'We won't be long. Lucy's all right.' He squeezed her arm. 'And you haven't eaten anything, remember? I promised you dinner last night and we ate nothing; I'd better get you some breakfast, before you fade away.'

'I don't think I'm in any danger of fading away.' She smiled.

'I'm not going to take any risks on that.' Mac held up a hand and summoned a taxi.

Melissa got in and looked out of the window as they were driven back to the strip. She remembered driving in here with Mac last night and it felt like an eternity ago.

They went into one of the nearest casinos. Melissa couldn't get over the fact that there were still a lot of people gambling at five-thirty in the morning. 'At least we don't feel conspicuous in our evening clothes,' she said to Mac as they took a seat in one of the coffee shops.

They ordered breakfast and the waitress brought them some coffee.

Mac watched Melissa. She looked so beautiful, her hair a glossy chestnut frame for her heart-shaped face. Her skin was pale, her eyes were tired, a heavy look in their violet-blue depths, as if the dark, thick eyelashes weighed them down.

She reached for her coffee, and the ring on her engagement finger caught the light and flashed with fierce intensity.

'Thanks for staying with me at the hospital,' he said gently.

'You wouldn't have been able to get rid of me if you'd tried.' She smiled at him, a faltering, shy smile that made his heart somersault in a very strange way. 'I'm just so relieved that Lucy is going to be all right.'

'Yes.' He leaned back in his seat and closed his eyes. 'It was a total nightmare, wasn't it?'

'But she's OK,' Melissa reminded him gently.

He opened his eyes and looked at her with direct, unwavering eyes. 'Yes, and now here we are sitting opposite each other in a restaurant. Back to where we were before that phone call.'

'It's a different restaurant.' She smiled. 'And I feel as if I've been through an emotional wringer since then.'

'Well, I feel as if someone has just given me a vicious wake-up call.' He shook his head.

'I suppose a health scare has that effect.'

'No, it's more than that.' Mac was emphatic, the dark eyes that held hers serious and intent. 'I watched you tonight at the hospital, noticed how you looked at Lucy. All I could think was how much I've been deceiving myself recently. I've thought that I could have it all,' he said disparagingly. 'My career, my child—and juggle everything perfectly on my own. But I can't. Tonight made me realise that.' He sighed. 'I'm not making much sense, am I?' He raked a hand through his hair distractedly. 'I feel as if I know in my heart what I want to say to you, Melissa, but my lips won't form the words.'

She swallowed hard as he reached across and took hold of her hand.

'I can't tell you how grateful I am to you, for all you've done for me recently—'

'You don't need to say that, Mac.'

'Yes, I do. I've dragged you into this…phoney situation. I've talked about my career, my child…' He shook his head. 'In fact I've been damn selfish.'

'I think you're being a bit hard on yourself,' she said quietly, her eyes moving over his face.

'Not really, because I'm probably running true to form now.'

'True to form?'

'I find myself selfishly wanting to hold on to you.'

'Do you?' Her senses were in turmoil now. She didn't know what to think. This was what she wanted, for him to say that he wanted her…and yet was it? Didn't she really want to hear, I love you?

'You told me tonight that, as much as you still love Simon, you won't go back to him. Is that true?'

She frowned, 'Mac, I—'

'The thing is that, thanks to this new contract, money isn't any object. I can afford to give you the best of everything…'

'Mac, what exactly are you saying to me?'

He met her eyes steadily across the table. 'I'm saying, I know you love Lucy, but will you give love a chance to grow between us?'

'You want us to start a relationship?'

His fingers caressed over her hand. 'I'm saying that I would feel very honoured if you would consider moving in with me,' he whispered huskily.

She stared at him, totally stunned by the words. 'I don't know what to say…'

'Then don't say anything; just think about it. I'm very

serious, Melissa. In fact, I've never been more serious.'
His eyes were intent on her face.

'Tonight you gave me a list of things you are looking
for in a man, remember? Someone who thinks you're special, someone who really cares about you. Someone to
restore your faith in men, and be there for you.'

She flushed as he repeated her words so precisely. 'You
were paying attention,' she murmured, with some embar-
rassment. 'I can't believe that I said that.'

'Well, you did, and I was hanging on your every word.'
He grinned. Then he looked at her with intense seriousness. 'If you give me a chance, I think I could fit your
requirements.'

She smiled. 'You make it sound like a commercial enterprise.'

'Maybe a relationship should be viewed in that light:
each person bringing something to a relationship that the
other person wants, creating something perfect in the pro-
cess.'

'Oh, yes?' Melissa grinned. She didn't know how to
look at this. But at least he seemed to want her. 'Problem
is, nothing is perfect.'

'Well, we already know that we are sexually compatible;
isn't that a good place to start?'

'You want me for physical pleasure?' She looked at him
wryly.

'I just want you.'

She closed her eyes on the wave of red-hot need those
words stirred inside her.

'I have this feeling that we'd make a good team,' he
said softly.

'I don't know, Mac. This is all a bit sudden—'

'Just think about it; that's all I ask.'

She looked at him then, her eyes moving over the handsome contours of his face—a face that had become so beloved to her over these last few days.

How she had got so deeply involved so quickly, she didn't know. All she did know was that she loved him, and, whether he loved her or not, she felt she had to give his proposition some very serious thought.

CHAPTER TWELVE

MELISSA surveyed her handiwork, but only half her mind was on the plants; the other half was very firmly on Mac.

'Hi, Melissa.'

Melissa turned and stood up as she saw Kurt hurrying over towards her.

'How's it going?'

'Fine. I'm just about finished in fact.' She shielded her eyes from the sun and looked up at her boss, a tall, good-looking man in his late thirties.

'You've done a good job with Schofield's garden,' he said, glancing around.

'Thanks. I must admit I'm pleased with it myself.'

'Is Schofield in?' Kurt nodded towards the house.

'No. He's in Vegas.' Melissa pulled her gloves off, her mind on Mac. She hadn't wanted to come back without him, but he had insisted, said there wasn't much point in her staying while he was spending all the time at the hospital. 'It's not as if it's an emergency any longer,' he had said calmly. 'Lucy is fine now. They are just keeping her in for a day's observation. J.B. and Nancy will understand that you've got to get back for work.'

It was two days since she had last seen Mac. He had driven her to McCarran Airport. 'I mean it, Melissa,' he had said steadily as he held her in his arms to say goodbye. 'Pack up at your apartment and move in with Lucy and me…'

Then he had put the keys of his Mercedes in her hand. 'Drive yourself home from the airport. My front-door key is on there as well. Let yourself in, wander around, make yourself at home.'

'Mac, I haven't said that I'll move in,' she had reminded him softly. 'I have to give this some serious thought.'

'I know, and I won't pressure you.'

Things had moved so quickly, she was still dazed by the speed of it. This was everything she could have dreamed of, and yet… A little part of her, the sensible part, wondered if all this sudden need Mac had for her was just part of some delayed shock from having thought he had nearly lost Lucy.

'When will he be back?' Kurt asked now. 'I just wanted to ask if he was happy with the garden and have a chat before I give him the bill.'

'This afternoon.'

Kurt nodded, then hesitated. 'Listen, I'm probably talking out of turn, but I've got the impression that you have been offered another job.'

'Have you?' Melissa looked up at him now, focussing sharply. 'Who told you that?'

'Simon Wesley wandered into the garden centre yesterday looking for you. He mentioned, in a roundabout way, a new project he had on the go in Vegas.'

'I see.' That was typical of Simon, she thought ruefully. Couldn't keep his mouth closed.

'Is it true?'

'Well…yes.'

'Hell, Melissa, you can't go.' Kurt sounded totally panic-stricken. 'Listen, I've got some very exciting projects lined up here. I really need your expertise.'

'Kurt, I—' She was going to say that she had met with Simon last night and had turned down his job.

'I'll give you a raise,' Kurt cut in quickly before she had a chance to say anything.

'Will you?' Melissa dusted her hands off on her jeans. 'In that case I'll stay,' she said with a grin.

Melissa was feeling extremely pleased with herself as she later set off to pick Mac up from the airport. She'd finished the garden, her finances had taken an upward swing, and Mac was coming home. Everything seemed to be falling into place nicely.

She felt confident now that she would get a bank loan to help her mother. And even if she didn't move in straight away with Mac, took things slowly, at least he wanted a relationship with her. It was cause for celebration.

Melissa parked the Mercedes and checked her reflection in the driving mirror.

She had gone home before coming to the airport and had taken some time and trouble with her appearance. Her make-up was flawless, her hair sat in a gleaming, silky frame around her face. So why did she feel nervous suddenly about seeing Mac again?

She got out of the car and walked towards the terminal.

Then, suddenly, she saw him coming out of the building. Tall and handsome in his jeans and T-shirt. He was holding Lucy in one arm, her pram and overnight case in the other.

'Mac.' She ran over towards him. 'Are you early, or am I late?'

'We're early.' For just a second their eyes held in a meaningful, loaded look.

The doubts that had tormented Melissa since she'd come home seemed to disappear.

'It's good to see you,' he said huskily.

'I'm glad you're back.' She smiled, then looked at Lucy. 'So, how are you?' she asked the baby, stroking Lucy's curls back from her face and looking down at her. 'What did the doctor say?'

'Just what he said before. It was a virus. A particularly bad one, but she's one very healthy little girl now. Well over it all.' Mac handed her across to Melissa as she gave him his car keys. 'Where did you park the car?'

'Just over there.' Melissa nodded behind her. 'Don't worry, your Merc is still in one piece.' She grinned. 'I'm

very relieved to be able to tell you that. I was a bit apprehensive driving it.'

'It's a dream to drive—I told you.'

'I never doubted that,' she said wryly. 'It's just that it's
not mine, and it's gorgeous.'

'Hey.' He put a finger under her chin, lifting it so that
he could look into her eyes. 'It's a family car. And I'm
hoping that you're going to be part of the family now,
remember?'

His lips met hers in a piercingly sweet kiss which took
her breath away. 'Come on,' he murmured, a seductive
tone in his voice. 'Let's get home.'

Melissa felt her emotions sing. Everything was going to
be all right. Mac hadn't asked her to move in with him on
a whim. He'd really thought about it and meant it.

'So how are things?' Mac asked her once they were out
on the highway.

'Great.'

He nodded. 'Nancy was all for ringing you last night.
She and J.B. are coming home themselves at the end of
the week and she wanted to know if we would make up a
foursome and have dinner with them.'

'Sounds fun.'

'Good.' Mac smiled. 'I had to go all out to stop her
phoning the house late last night. I took the phone from
her and dialled the number of your apartment instead. But
you were out anyway.'

'I had dinner with Simon last night. He was trying to
talk me into accepting his job.'

Mac allowed himself to take his eyes off the fast flowing
lanes of traffic to glance at her for just a second. 'Did you
give him an answer?'

'I told him I didn't want to move to Vegas.' She shook
her head. 'But I had already told him that on the phone
and he didn't seem to want to accept it then either.'

Mac was silent. He wasn't happy about her having dinner with Simon whilst he was away. He wondered if he should tell her. He imagined the words in his head. I don't want you socialising with Simon Wesley. Don't do it again. Maybe not; it sounded a bit heavy-handed, and he wasn't the type to be jealously possessive. He tried to put the feelings away as he turned off the busy highway and onto the quieter roads leading up towards his house.

'I've made some progress with the garden while you've been away,' she told him casually.

'I can't wait to see it.' Now that they were on a quiet road, he slowed and reached to take her hand in his. 'You're not wearing your ring,' he said, running a hand over the naked finger.

The touch of his skin against hers gave a warm glow of anticipation. 'It's at the jewellers. They're adjusting the size for me.' She had wondered if he wanted her to continue wearing it on her engagement finger. Maybe she had her answer now; it sounded as if he did.

'When will you pick it up?'

'I don't know. Tomorrow, I suppose.' She looked over at him with a frown. 'Don't worry, I'll put it back on my finger before we go out with Nancy and J.B.'

He nodded and released her to pull the car onto his driveway beside her pick-up.

The niggles of doubt were back. Were J.B. and Nancy the only reason he had asked about the ring?

Mac carried Lucy into the house, leaving the pram and luggage until later.

He went into the lounge and opened up the sliding glass doors to look out onto the garden.

The difference was spectacular. Plants in containers adorned the sides of the decking. Creepers of honeysuckle and roses were intertwined over the trellis, leading the eye to the profusion of colour in the garden beyond.

'I chose plants that were already fairly well-established, to give the garden maturity. I thought as you're not ex-

actly…the patient type you might prefer the instant garden.' Melissa watched him, waiting for his reaction.

'It's beautiful, Melissa, truly beautiful.' He looked
across at her. 'Almost as lovely as you,' he murmured, his
eyes raking over her slender figure in the white sundress.
Lucy wriggled in his arms, diverting his attention.

'I think you're tired, aren't you, sweetheart?' he asked
her gently.

'Why don't you sort her out and unpack, while I make
us something to eat?' Melissa asked him.

'I've got a better idea. Why don't I see to Lucy while
you ring for a take-out and get dinner delivered?'

'Are you frightened of my cooking, Mac?' she asked
him teasingly. 'I know I once told you it wasn't a strong
point, but I can manage pasta, and I did some shopping
for you today.'

'Did you?' He leaned over and kissed her. 'I'll test out
your cooking skills another time,' he told her in a husky
undertone, against her ear. 'But I don't want you wasting
energy in the kitchen tonight.'

He smiled as he saw the flare of colour in her cheeks.

'There's a whole directory of restaurants that deliver,
plus some fast-food places—it's in a drawer in the kitchen.
Second from left, I think.' He hitched Lucy farther up on
his hip as she tried to escape from him. 'The French restaurant is pretty good, but I don't mind what you order.'

Mac disappeared upstairs and Melissa wandered through
to the kitchen.

The book with the telephone numbers was where Mac
had said it was, along with menus. She flicked through
them, then dialled and placed their order.

As she was replacing the book, she noticed a photograph
at the bottom of the drawer.

Curious, she pulled it out and looked more closely at it.
It was Mac, a younger, skinnier Mac, looking relaxed and

happy. But it wasn't Mac that held her attention, it was the woman he had his arm around.

She was very attractive, probably the same age as him, with long blonde hair, and very slender. Mac was looking down at her adoringly.

'That's Kay,' Mac said from behind her.

She whirled around. 'I'm sorry, I just saw it at the bottom of the drawer and was curious.' She wondered if she sounded as guilty as she felt.

'That's OK,' he said easily. He reached over and took the photo from her to glance at it for a minute.

'She's very pretty,' Melissa remarked.

'Yes. She is.' He put it back in the drawer and closed it. 'Did you order the food?'

She nodded. 'We've gone French.'

Discontented cries from upstairs made Mac turn. 'Better finish sorting Lucy out, before she tells me off in any louder terms,' he said with a grin. 'I won't be long. Open a bottle of wine.'

As Melissa sat out on the patio waiting for Mac, she tried to dismiss the photograph from her mind. Yet the image of Kay's face and the way Mac had been looking down at her stayed, disturbingly real, nagging at the back of her mind.

The sun was slowly sinking in a red haze over the sea when Mac joined her outside.

'Where's Lucy?'

'Fast asleep. Don't worry, she did have something to eat a little while ago. I think the journey has just exhausted her.'

Mac reached for the glass of white wine she had poured for him and held it up towards hers. 'Here's to us, and to the future.'

She met his eyes across the table. 'To us,' she said quietly.

A gentle breeze stirred the wind chimes that Melissa had

hung around the patio. It was a relaxing sound in the warm evening air.

'How's your mother?' he asked, leaning back into his chair and making himself comfortable.

'She's on good form. I rang her last night before going out.'

Melissa wondered if it was her imagination, or did the mention of last night bring an awkward silence for a moment?

Mac looked at her steadily across the table. 'Have you thought anything more about moving in with me?'

'Of course I have,' she said quietly. 'It's practically all I've thought about since arriving back.'

'Apart from the job in Vegas.' He raised an eyebrow as he looked at her.

'I've given that some thought as well.' She inclined her head. 'Offers like that don't come along very often.'

'You told Simon that you didn't want to move to Vegas, but you didn't tell him you didn't want the job.'

'It's the same thing, isn't it?' She shrugged. 'To be honest I would have accepted the job if it were here. It's an exciting project, plus good money.'

'Did you turn it down because of me?'

She smiled. 'Well, it would be hard for us to have any kind of a relationship if I was in Nevada and you were in California.'

'We could possibly work something out,' he said quietly. 'I don't want to uproot Lucy at this point; she's settled and her grandmother is nearby. But I don't want to stand in your way, Melissa. I know your career is important to you. Maybe you could come back at weekends, and I could see you when I go out on business mid-week. It's not beyond the realms of possibility.'

'Maybe…' Melissa didn't like the suggestion. She didn't want to be away from him all week. Long-distance romances were hard. Plus she had grown very attached to

Lucy. If she moved in with Mac, she wanted them to be a family.

The front doorbell rang. 'That will be tonight's dinner,' he said, getting up.

Melissa watched him walk away from her. If he was serious about her, would he really have suggested that she go to work with her ex-fiancé in Vegas all week?

The evening sun faded completely; the garden lights came on automatically, their subdued gleam twinkling over the glasses. They ate dinner and talked about nothing in particular for a while, and it was very pleasant.

Mac asked her about her childhood in Texas. He told her about his days growing up in the Napa Valley. His father had owned a vineyard and he had worked for him during the summer holidays.

'Where is your father now?'

'He's still there, with his vineyard. My parents divorced when I was thirteen.'

'It must have been tough going through a divorce at the age of thirteen,' she said softly.

'A bit grim,' he agreed. 'I vowed that if I ever had a child she would never have to go through the trauma of a marriage break-up.'

For a moment the sadness in his eyes made her long to reach out to him.

'But you never know what's around the corner, do you?' he finished wryly.

'No. Maybe it's a good job.'

He smiled.

Her eyes moved over his face, noting the shadows beneath his eyes from his recent sleepless nights with Lucy. If she could see into the future, would she see Kay walking back into his life? There was no doubt about it—Mac hadn't wanted that divorce. She was willing to bet he had fought like a tiger to save the marriage. The knowledge was disturbing.

She glanced away from him, trying to close out those thoughts. She didn't want to think like this. She wanted to sit here and revel in his company, reach out and kiss him, make love with him.

She glanced at her watch. Maybe she should distance herself. She was too emotionally undecided about Mac's feelings for her and, given the circumstances, it was best to play things safe.

'I should be going. I've got to get up early in the morning.'

He frowned. 'I was hoping you might like to stay.' His voice was warm and honeyed. It did incredibly disturbing things to her body.

'I don't think so, Mac,' she said, meeting his gaze, trying to keep a hint of reserve in her tone. 'I haven't brought my night things and—'

'You don't need night things, Melissa.' He smiled and stood up, then reached to take her hand so that he could bring her to her feet.

'I have a spare toothbrush in a drawer.' He fixed her with a teasing, attractive look.

She felt her heart thumping against her chest as he bent to kiss her. His lips were gentle against hers, then more demanding as she kissed him back.

She felt his hands, gentle against her back. Felt her body respond to him, wanting him, hungry for him.

'Will you stay?' he asked, drawing back.

She liked the way he didn't take it for granted that she would, even after the fire of her response.

Who was she kidding anyway? she asked herself. She was fighting a losing battle with her will-power. She wanted him to hold her—she couldn't get close enough to him. There was no way she really wanted to go home. 'Yes, Mac.' She whispered her acceptance huskily, and he turned to lead her upstairs.

Her stomach twisted into tight knots of longing as he kissed her again, laying her back against the bed.

Then they were undressing each other with a haste that made her breathless.

She felt his hands curving around her, stroking the length of her back, caressing her to fever pitch.

The cotton sheets were cool against her body. His body was lithe and agile against hers, his skin satin-smooth. Her hands moved over the powerful contours of his shoulders, stroking down over his back.

As he took possession of her, the world seemed to dissolve into hazy unreality, a mist of exploding passions and blissful satisfaction.

He just held her for a long time afterwards, his hand stroking her back.

They lay in silence. She closed her eyes, listening to the steady rhythm of his heart. Lying there with him was the most wonderful feeling. He didn't even need to speak—the tenderness in his touch filled the empty spaces of conversation.

Then she moved onto her side, cuddling closer, and the spell of quiet unreality was broken.

'That was wonderful.' He kissed the top of her head.

'Yes.' She opened her eyes and looked up at him. His face was in shadow, the room lit only by the lights that shone in from the landing.

If only he would tell her he loved her, she thought suddenly. She buried her head against his chest, trying to close out those thoughts.

His kisses were so warm and passionate, his arms so tender—how could three little words compare to those things?

But they did. They meant a lot. That was what was wrong. That was why she felt so unsure about this relationship. Mac was passionate and possessive when they made love, but there was something missing. Those three little words.

She cuddled closer, and squeezed her eyes tightly closed. Love would grow, she told herself forcefully. And anyway, she had enough of it for the two of them.

CHAPTER THIRTEEN

WHEN she woke in the morning, she was alone in bed. She turned as she heard the bedroom door open.

'A cup of tea,' Mac said, putting it down on the bedside table.

'Thanks.' She rolled over to look at him, brushing her hair out of her eyes. She noticed that he was dressed in his suit. 'What time is it?'

'Almost seven-thirty.' He sat down on the side of the bed and reached to kiss her.

His lips were warm and erotic. She smiled sleepily as he pulled away. 'I don't suppose you can come back to bed?'

'I'd like to,' he grinned, and stroked her hair away from her face with a tender hand. 'Unfortunately, work is calling. I've got to go into the office today.'

She sat up, pulling the sheets up firmly over her naked body as she reached for her tea.

'Patricia will be here in fifteen minutes.'

Melissa grimaced. 'I'd better get up and make myself scarce.'

'Why?'

'I don't want to shock her.'

Mac laughed at that. 'I'm a grown man, Melissa. I don't think your presence will shock dear Patricia. She's a married lady with three grown children of her own.'

He bent to kiss her again, his lips sensual against hers.

The sound of the front door opening and Patricia's cheerful voice calling hello made him pull away. 'Better go,' he said ruefully. 'Listen, there's something for you on the dressing table. Take it before you leave.'

'Oh?' She sat up to look at the dressing table but couldn't see anything. 'What is it?'

'Look when I've gone.' He kissed her again. 'Oh, and do you think you could do me a favour and ring Nancy some time today? Tell her that dinner next week is fine.'

'OK.' Melissa nodded.

'Thanks. I was thinking maybe we could invite them here instead of going out? It would look good, wouldn't it? I'll ask Patricia if she wouldn't mind cooking.'

'If you want.'

After he had gone, Melissa frowned. Why had Mac said that inviting Nancy and J.B. here would 'look good?' It gave her an uneasy feeling, as if he was still thinking about their union in terms of his career.

She dismissed the notion and threw the covers off the bed to climb out. Probably Mac just wanted to repay his employers for their generosity over the weekend.

She wrapped herself in Mac's dressing gown and went for a shower in the *en-suite* bathroom.

It wasn't until she came back into the bedroom that she remembered Mac telling her that there was something for her on the dressing table. She went across to have a look.

An envelope lay there with her name on it.

Frowning, she picked it up and opened it. There was a cheque inside for an amount that made her gasp.

She sat down on the stool and just stared down at the piece of paper. It was generous, over-generous in fact.

Was that what she was to him? An accessory he could bring out at business occasions and keep happy with a cheque?

She felt deeply insulted. Before she could think any further about it, she tore the paper into tiny pieces and left them on the glass top of the dressing table.

Then she got dressed and went downstairs.

She was surprised to see that Mac was still in the kitchen. He was talking to Patricia. Lucy was sitting in her high chair drinking some juice. She held her hands out towards Melissa.

'Hello, darling.' Melissa reached and kissed the little upturned face.

'Would you like coffee, Melissa?' Patricia asked.

Melissa smiled at her. 'No, thank you. I've got to get to work.' She avoided looking at Mac, but instead turned her attention back to Lucy. She looked the picture of health.

'She looks fine, doesn't she?' Patricia remarked. 'Hard to believe that she was so ill.'

'Yes, it is.' Melissa kissed the child again.

Sweet and lovely Lucy. Melissa's heart went out to the child. She loved her very much. 'I'd better go.' She pulled herself away.

'Yes, me, too.' Mac put his coffee cup down and went across to kiss Lucy. He picked up his briefcase. 'See you later, Pat.'

He followed Melissa out through the house.

'Thanks for your cheque,' she said quietly. 'But I can't accept it.'

'Why not?'

She looked around at him then. 'Under the rules of our deception, I thought I made it clear that I didn't want payment.'

'That's not payment,' he said firmly. 'It's a gift. Look, I know you're worried about your mother, and I can help. It's as simple as that.'

'It's very generous of you.' She opened her handbag to look for her car keys. 'But actually I have my finances sorted out. Kurt has given me a big raise.'

'And you don't want to be under an obligation?' he said softly. 'It's all right, Melissa. There are no strings attached to the money.'

His mobile phone started to ring and he took it out of his pocket. 'That will be the office.' He glared at the instrument. 'I've got to go, Melissa. We'll talk about this later.'

'Yes, OK.' She watched as he walked away, answering the call as he got into his Mercedes.

She remembered their conversation in Vegas when he had asked her to move in with him. 'You make it sound like a commercial enterprise,' she had said.

He had made no attempt to deny it.

Where were her damn keys? She scrabbled frantically in her bag. She heard Mac say, 'Oh, hi, J.B. This is a surprise. Yes, she's fine…and Melissa, yes. She was just going to ring Nancy today.'

Then he backed the car off the drive and waved at her as he drove away.

Her keys definitely weren't in her bag. Melissa returned to the house.

Patricia was singing along to the radio as she loaded the dishwasher. Lucy was scribbling on a drawing pad, looking very industrious.

Patricia turned the radio down as she saw Melissa.

'Sorry to disturb you, Patricia—I've mislaid my keys.' Melissa's eyes searched over the counter tops and located them by the stove. 'There they are.'

'Mac was asking me this morning if I'd cook for a dinner party he wants to throw next week,' Patricia told her cheerfully. 'I said Thursday would be good for me, if that's all right with you?'

'That's fine.' Melissa picked up the keys and turned with a smile. 'Thanks, Patricia.'

'I don't mind at all.' Patricia closed the dishwasher and turned to pour herself another coffee. 'In fact I must admit I felt a lifting of my spirits when he told me he was giving a dinner party here. I haven't helped him cater for anything like that since Kay left.'

Melissa hesitated. 'You've known Mac a long time, haven't you?'

'Yes.' Patricia smiled at her. 'Long before he married Kay. It's nice to see him putting his life back together, throwing dinner parties again. Because everything in his life has been strictly business or family since she left. He's obviously put the past behind him at last.'

'Yes, obviously.' Melissa forced a bright smile to her face, but inside her heart was sore. Had anything changed? 'I'd better go or I'll be late for work.' With a last glance over at Lucy, Melissa headed for the door.

When Melissa got home from work that evening, Mac was waiting for her. He was sitting on the swing chair on the front porch, looking quite at home and very smart in beige trousers and matching shirt.

By contrast, she felt dishevelled after her long day.

'This is a surprise,' she said as she went up the front path. 'Where's Lucy?'

'Mom arrived just as I got back from work...insisted on taking her. I thought maybe you'd like to go out for dinner?'

'That would be nice.' She opened her front door and led the way inside. 'Let me have a shower and freshen up. I won't be long.'

'OK. Do you want me to fix you a drink?'

'Yes, please,' she called back from the bedroom. 'I'd love a glass of wine. There's some in the fridge.'

She stripped off, glad to get out of the shorts and T-shirt. Then she walked into her bathroom and stood under the forceful jet of the shower. It was a blissful feeling. Totally invigorating. As she stood there, she tried to think what she should say to Mac. She felt sure he was going to want an answer tonight about whether or not she'd move in with him. And she had to clear some things up. She needed to know exactly what he wanted from the relationship. If it was a convenient arrangement, a live-in lover, someone to help him with Lucy, then he should tell her in plain English. And maybe she should throw away her pride and tell him how she was feeling. She had never been one for keeping her emotions locked up. This was something new for her.

When she stepped out of the shower, she felt a lot better. She wrapped herself in a towel and tied another towel, turban-style, around her hair.

Mac was in the bedroom when she went through. 'Your wine,' he said, putting it down on the table.

'Thanks.' Now that she was face to face with him, her brave, clear words seemed to disappear. He had this effect on her, she realised suddenly. She was scared of losing him. Scared of coming on too strong in case it would make him back away from her.

He caught her by the hand as she turned away. 'Have you forgiven me about the cheque?'

'It was very tactless of you, Mac,' she said quietly. 'I told you I didn't want money.'

'Maybe it was clumsy of me. But I just wanted to help—'

'Not maybe, it *was* clumsy.' She looked up at him.

'When someone you care about is worried and you know you can fix the problem for them, it's very difficult to stand by and do nothing Melissa.'

He cared about her, but he didn't love her. She noted his careful wording. 'I know you have good intentions, but I'm sorry, Mac, it's too much money and I couldn't accept it.'

He frowned. 'OK, have it your way.'

'But thanks for the offer,' she said softly.

'Sure.'

She sat down on the edge of the bed and he crouched down beside her and took hold of her hand. 'You've got a critical case of cold feet about moving in with me, haven't you?' he asked softly.

She smiled at him then. 'Does it show that much?'

He nodded. 'Get dressed and we'll go out, discuss this over a quiet drink and some dinner.'

'I'd like that.' Her eyes moved over his face. He looked so sincere, so earnest that she wanted to put her arms around him.

'Well, if we stay here I'm going to want to make love to you,' he murmured, his eyes drifting down to where the towel dipped slightly, revealing the silky curves of her figure. 'And that's not going to solve anything, is it?'

Melissa hesitated and then smiled. 'It might for a few hours.'

'But I want more than a few hours, Melissa; that's the trouble.' He stood up and moved away from her.

Melissa had hardly said two words since getting into the car. Mac glanced sideways at her. She looked very beautiful, the flowered print of her blue dress complementing the honeyed tones of her skin. Her dark hair sat glossily in place. She seemed serene and relaxed. But Mac knew that wasn't the case. Just one look at those gorgeous violet-blue eyes and he knew he was in trouble. She was going to end things between them; he could feel it.

He pulled into the restaurant car park overlooking the wide sweep of a creamy beach, and they went inside.

It was a popular place, and very busy for so early. Melissa found a vacant seat in an alcove by one of the picture windows, and Mac went to the bar to get them a drink while they waited for a table.

Melissa's eyes moved idly over the interior. It was stylish yet dark, the main attraction being its wonderful views, and presumably the food. Her eyes moved to Mac. In all honesty the last thing on her mind at the moment was food. Maybe they should have gone somewhere else, somewhere quieter, to talk.

Mac came back to the table with their drinks. 'It will be about half an hour before we can eat; is that all right?'

'Yes, I guess so.'

He sat down beside her. Ask him, she told herself. Ask him if he still loves Kay. She formulated the words in her mind and opened her mouth. 'How did work go today?'

'OK. But it is getting a bit heavy at the moment. I've got to fly up to Vegas again tomorrow. There's a big meeting with the directors of the company.'

A crowd of people came through from the restaurant and the babble of noise and laughter was even louder.

'Maybe you'd prefer to go somewhere else...' Mac trailed off as he caught sight of someone.

Melissa followed his gaze towards a slender woman wearing a grey trouser suit. She turned and smiled. 'Mac! Fancy seeing you here!'

'Hello, Kay.' He stood up as she walked across towards him.

Melissa felt sick inside suddenly. That they should bump into Mac's ex-wife now, of all times, seemed incredible. She wondered if someone up above was playing a joke on her, or maybe trying to tell her something. You made a mistake with Simon: don't do it again. The words played over in her head, mocking her.

Looking at Kay, Melissa could understand why Mac would be besotted by her. The photograph that she had seen hadn't done her justice. Kay was more than just beautiful; she was stunningly attractive. Her blonde hair was cut short now, and it framed a face that had classical good looks, high cheekbones and wide green eyes.

'I'm glad I've bumped into you; it gives me a chance to thank you for your advice last week,' she said, reaching to kiss him on the cheek.

'It went all right, then?'

'Yes.' She smiled. 'Like a dream. The guy was most apologetic.'

'I'm sure he was. You're a talented architect, and it wasn't your mistake.'

'Yeah...well.' She smiled at him. 'Thanks for believing in me, anyway.' She glanced over at Melissa.

'Kay, this is Melissa.' Mac introduced them smoothly.

Kay nodded, then immediately turned her attention back to Mac. 'How's Lucy?'

'She's fine now.'

'Good. These viruses can strike without warning, I believe. It sounds like it was very worrying.'

'Yes. It was. Come over and see her if you want—'

'I will if I have time, Mac. But you know my schedule is pretty hectic.'

'Yes, I know.'

She smiled at him and then dropped her voice huskily. 'It brings back happy memories seeing you in here.' Then, with another smile in Melissa's direction, she left them.

'Sorry about that.' Mac sat back down.

'That's OK.' Melissa reached for her drink. She felt she needed one. 'You told her about Lucy being ill, I take it?'

'Yes. I rang her from Vegas. I thought she should know.'

'And hoped she might dash to her bedside?'

'I hoped it might stimulate some kind of concern for her daughter.' He shook his head and for a moment his eyes were distant. 'I should have known better.'

'Why does it bring back happy memories for Kay to see you in here?'

'We used to meet here sometimes, after work. My old firm was just around the corner.'

Melissa watched him and felt a dull ache somewhere deep inside. What was it he had said to her in Vegas? That even though you knew you couldn't go back it didn't stop you loving someone.

She looked away from him towards the window, trying to gather her strength and her courage to do what she knew she had to do.

The late afternoon sun sparkled over the water. There was a pink glow in the sky as the sun started to dip.

'Anyway, we haven't come here to talk about my ex-wife.' Mac looked over at her. 'I had a front-door key cut for you today,' he said. 'It was probably very cavalier of me, seeing as you haven't given me your answer yet.' He took a silver key from his pocket and held it in the palm of his hand.

She looked at him then, and felt her eyes swim for a moment with a haze of sudden tears.

'I can't move in with you, Mac,' she said softly. It took all her will-power to say those words. 'I just can't.'

His hand closed over the key. 'I know it's a big step. We'd both be crazy not to be a bit apprehensive, but please think again, Melissa. I realise that you have a lot to be wary about. You'll be taking on someone else's child. Not an easy task.' He reached to touch her hand. 'Is it Lucy that worries you?'

'Partly,' she admitted hesitantly.

'I'm not looking to delegate any of my responsibilities for her, you know—'

'I know that.' She shook her head. 'And anyway I'd feel honoured to share some of the responsibilities for Lucy. It's not that.'

He met her eyes seriously. 'So what is it?'

She looked away and down at her hands. 'This morning, when you left that money for me, I was so angry. And when I started to really deliberate deeply about us all I could think was that you had got carried away with all this damn deception—that you were really just looking for a convenient partner, someone to grace your business dinners, be at your side at functions, and be Lucy's mother—that's all you need. And I…well, I'd got carried away with it all, too. I was looking for stability, for a feeling of belonging. For love,' she admitted ruefully. 'Oh, I know you said it might grow between us, but that seems like an awfully big gamble, Mac. And meanwhile my emotions where Lucy is concerned are getting more and more involved. I love her, Mac; I looked at her sitting at the breakfast table this morning and I thought how much I wanted her in my life, how much she means to me. Walking away from her is the hardest thing I'll ever do in my life.'

'Then don't walk away,' he said huskily.

'I have to.' She whispered the words unsteadily. 'Because loving Lucy isn't enough. Don't you see—the longer I play at being your partner, the more involved I'm getting? One day you're going to turn around to me and you're going to say, This isn't working, Melissa. And I'm going to be devastated. I'm going to have to leave a little girl that I've given my heart and soul to.'

'Why would I say that?' Mac asked quietly.

'I don't know. Because you've found true love...maybe Kay will want to come back to you. Let's face it, maybe one day she's going to turn around and think about what she has lost.'

'Now you are in the realm of fantasy.'

'Am I?' Melissa shook her head. 'Look, we've both got caught up in a deception, got carried away with all the pretence. We don't really love each other; that's the bottom line.'

'So what are you going to do? Give Simon Wesley another chance?' His voice hardened.

'I don't know what I'm going to do.' She stood up. 'I just know that it isn't going to work out between us. I'll have to go now. Don't worry about me; I'll get a cab home.'

'Melissa, don't go.'

'I have to.' She glanced back at him once, but he was a blurred image as her eyes filled with tears.

Outside, the sun was going down in a ball of red flames on the horizon. It was a tranquil scene, and one that was very welcome after the emotion that had torn her apart.

On impulse she went down the steps to the shore, deciding to walk for a while. She'd done the right thing, she kept telling herself.

So why did she feel as if her heart would never mend?

CHAPTER FOURTEEN

THE decision to go to Florida to see her mother had come to her as she had tossed and turned, unable to sleep. She needed to escape. Kurt owed her some holidays and, as Mac's garden was finished, she could ask for them now.

'Are you coming back?' Kurt looked suspicious when she went in with the request the next morning. 'You're not going to Vegas, are you?'

Under ordinary circumstances Melissa would have been amused by his questions. But she was too tired, too upset to even think about it. 'I'm going to see my mother in Miami.'

Kurt looked relieved. 'OK. Just leave the telephone number, in case I want to check with you about anything, will you?'

Melissa would have left her soul if it meant she could get away faster. So it was that, less than twenty-four hours after she had finished with Mac, she was on her way to the airport, a seat booked and her mother expecting her.

She'd have to forget Mac, she told herself as she climbed into the cab. She'd got along without him before; she would now. She closed her eyes and leaned back against the seat.

She was a strong, independent woman and she had no room in her life for a man who couldn't return her love completely. The words felt good. She'd gone through enough with Simon; she couldn't face that again. She had to take control of her life, fall for someone safe next time.

Except she didn't want anyone else. And maybe safe was boring.

She opened her eyes just as they were passing the mall

where she had left her ring to be altered. She should have picked it up this morning.

She'd leave it. It was a reminder of something she wanted to forget, wasn't it?

She sat forward. 'Excuse me, but do you think you could stop here for a moment?'

The driver didn't look too pleased, but he did as she asked.

'I won't be a moment. There's something I've forgotten,' Melissa said, climbing out hurriedly.

She had little time to get to the airport, but she stood and waited to be served.

'It's a lovely ring,' the jeweller remarked as he handed it to her across the counter.

'Yes, it is.' Melissa slid it back onto her finger. It fitted perfectly. She stared down at its sparkle and intensity and thought about Mac and how much she loved him. How much she wished he loved her.

'I hope you have it well insured?'

'Insured?' Melissa looked up. 'I didn't think that was necessary with a cubic zircon. It's just got sentimental value more than anything else.'

'A cubic zircon?' The man looked at her as if she was mad. 'It's a flawless diamond.'

'It can't be.' Melissa stared at him. 'Are you sure?'

'Of course I'm sure,' the jeweller said, a stiff, reproving note in his voice. 'I've been in the trade long enough to recognise a gem of such good quality when I see it.'

She took it off her finger and put it back in its box. Now she was totally confused. 'It's just to make things a bit more authentic…' Mac had said. 'Look on it as a stage prop.'

All the way to the airport she puzzled over the ring. Why would he give her a flawless diamond? There had to be some sort of catch.

She was cutting it fine to catch her flight. She only just

had time to check her bag in at the desk and run for the gate. She felt as if she was acting on remote control, as if her body was going through the motions of what was expected of it, yet her mind was on a different planet.

The flight attendants went through safety procedures. The aircraft thundered to the end of the runway and left the ground. Melissa took out the ring box and opened it for a closer inspection.

It was a fantastic ring.

'Well, at least you've still got the ring,' a deeply familiar voice grated beside her.

She looked up in shock, almost dropping the box. Mac was standing in the aisle. For a moment she could only stare up at him, wondering if he was a figment of her fevered imagination.

The woman who was sitting next to her also stared up at him, a look of admiration in her eyes as she took in the tall, handsome man in the dark suit. He smiled at her. 'Would you mind changing places with me?' he asked politely. 'I'm just in the seat behind yours.'

The woman smiled back at him. 'No, I don't mind at all.'

'What are you doing here?' Melissa whispered urgently as he slid into the seat beside her.

'I'm going to Miami,' Mac said calmly.

'What, on business?' Melissa had never been more perplexed in her life. She wondered if she had fallen asleep and this was all a dream.

Mac nodded. 'The most important business trip of my life.'

Melissa tried to think calmly. 'Shouldn't you be in Vegas?' She clamped her hand across her mouth in horror. 'Mac! You've got a really important meeting in Vegas. It's with the directors of the company—'

'I don't care.'

Melissa stared at him. 'What do you mean, you don't

care? Of course you do. It's your career; it's tremendously important to you.' Her eyes narrowed. 'It's the reason you got involved with me in the first place.'

'You know, that's what I thought as well.' Mac nodded. His manner was infuriatingly calm, irritatingly vague. 'Then you finished with me yesterday, and suddenly a few things fell into place.'

'What things?'

'You accused me yesterday of getting carried away with our deception. You were right.'

'I know I was right.'

'I made all those little rules up, didn't I?' Mac continued. 'Don't get involved with Simon being foremost on my list, and then I got you the ring…the stage prop.'

'The jeweller said it was a flawless diamond.'

'Yes, it is.'

'You led me to believe that it was a fake.'

'No, I didn't. You assumed it was a fake.'

'Why would you buy me a flawless diamond?' She looked down at the sparkle of the gem and remembered him handing it to her on that flight to Vegas.

'I told myself that you were putting yourself out for me. You were wonderful, and I wanted you to have the best damn ring I could buy.'

'You'll have to have it back.'

'I don't want it back. If anything, I want to put time back to when I first gave it to you.'

'Mac, I don't understand.'

'I love you, Melissa,' he said quietly. 'I don't want to spend another day, or night, without you.'

Her eyes glazed over with tears. 'No, you don't,' she said shakily. 'You just want me to come to your business dinner next Thursday and pretend—'

'To hell with the business dinner next Thursday,' he grated rawly. 'I don't care about that. I do care about you.'

She stared at him, trying to take in his words.

'Don't you see? I've been lying to myself, telling myself that our little deception was all for J.B. and Nancy. But it wasn't.'

'It wasn't?'

'The person I was deceiving the most was me. I told myself that I needed you around because of my job. But in reality I just wanted you around. I told myself the ring was a prop. But I wanted you to have the best...I was lying to myself even as I bought it. The truth is that I love you, Melissa, I adore you...I'm crazy about you.'

'But you still love Kay.' Melissa's voice was very unsteady. She wanted so much to believe what he was saying to her, yet she was frightened of being hurt, being disappointed.

'No, I don't.'

'You were devastated when she left you. You've never got over it,' Melissa told him firmly.

Mac shook his head. 'Yes, I was devastated by the divorce. For one thing, I'd promised myself from a young age that no child of mine would ever suffer a broken home. Then it happened and I had no control over it and that was a dreadful, dreadful feeling.

'I felt like I was letting Lucy down. That was my main sorrow. If the truth be told, Kay and I had grown apart. I think that's why I can be friends with her so easily now. There are just no sentiments of love left.'

Melissa stared at him. 'And that's honestly how you really feel?'

'Yes.' He frowned. 'Melissa, I know I don't have a lot to offer. I've a little girl who desperately needs a mother figure in her life and I'm not the most wonderful person when it comes to finding the right words. But I love you more than I've ever loved a woman in my life. I'm not going to walk away from you because I've found true love, or because Kay wants to come back—that's ludicrous, because you are my true love. Please reconsider, and come back to me.'

'Oh, Mac.' Suddenly she was in his arms, being cradled against his chest.

'I know you still have feelings for Simon. But I'll try so hard to make you happy, Melissa.'

She pulled back and looked up at him. 'That's ridiculous—I was over Simon almost from the first moment I looked into your eyes.' She whispered the words unsteadily. 'I love you, Mac. I love you so much it hurts. Meeting you made me realise what a mistake I would have made if I'd married anyone else.'

He looked astonished. 'So why did you finish with me, then?'

'Because I thought you were still biding your time, hoping that you would patch things up with Kay—that I was just an accessory. Hell, Mac, you never said you loved me. You even told me that you didn't mind if I went to work in Las Vegas, that you'd just see me at the weekend.'

'I was trying to be reasonable. At that point I felt that if I over-played my hand and came down too possessively I'd lose you completely to Simon.' He stroked a tender finger down the side of her face. 'And maybe I was a bit wary of saying "I love you" in case it all went wrong. I was worried a lot about Lucy getting too attached to you as well. I didn't think I could cope with her broken heart as well as my own. I'd made one mistake in my life; I was terrified of making it two. But when you walked away from me yesterday I knew, beyond any doubt, that if I let you go that would be the worst mistake of my life. I chased after you...but you'd gone. Then I tried sitting outside your house, but you didn't come home and I had to get back for Lucy.'

'I spent a while walking, trying to get my head cleared.'

'Then I had a hell of a job finding you today. I left a message on your answering machine.'

'I didn't see it. But then, I've been dashing around a lot, trying to organise this trip at the last minute. How did you find me?' She sat back and looked at him in puzzlement. 'And who is looking after Lucy?'

He smiled. 'Patricia said she'd stay until I got back. I rang Kurt, thinking you'd be at work today, and he told me you were going to Miami. I had to practically threaten him to get your mother's number. Then I had a hell of a job getting your mother to tell me what flight you were booked on. She wanted to know my intentions towards her daughter.'

'And what are your intentions?' Melissa asked breathlessly.

'Strictly honourable. No hint of any deception in sight,' he assured her solemnly. 'When I got to the airport no one would tell me if you were booked on the flight or not. So the only way to find out was to get on the flight myself.'

'And here you are,' she said happily, 'when you should be in Vegas.'

He shrugged. 'They say Miami is nice at this time of year.' Then he leaned closer and kissed her slowly, passionately until her heart felt as if it was running a race. 'Melissa, I never loved Kay the way I love you,' he said huskily as he pulled back. 'I adore you. I know that you're still unsure about us, but I want you so much…'

She saw the warmth, the love in his eyes. 'I'm not unsure any more,' she breathed softly. 'And I think, if the offer is still open, that I would very much like to move in with you after all.'

Their lips met in a deep, passionate kiss. It was a long time before Mac could pull away, could look down at her.

'The offer comes with conditions now,' he said gently, firmly.

'What kind of conditions?' She looked up at him, puzzled.

'I want you to do me the honour of becoming my wife,' he said gently.

She watched as he opened the ring box, and then looked at her. 'This is what I should have done on that flight to Vegas.'

'I'll second that.' She reached to kiss him, her heart in that kiss.

MILLS & BOON®

Makes any time special™

Mills & Boon publish 29 new titles every month. Select from...

Modern Romance™   Tender Romance™

Sensual Romance™

Medical Romance™ Historical Romance™

MAT2

FREE!

4 Books
and a surprise gift!

We would like to take this opportunity to thank you for reading this Mills & Boon® book by offering you the chance to take FOUR more specially selected titles from the Modern Romance™ series absolutely FREE! We're also making this offer to introduce you to the benefits of the Reader Service™—

- ★ FREE home delivery
- ★ FREE gifts and competitions
- ★ FREE monthly Newsletter
- ★ Books available before they're in the shops
- ★ Exclusive Reader Service discounts

Accepting these FREE books and gift places you under no obligation to buy; you may cancel at any time, even after receiving your free shipment. Simply complete your details below and return the entire page to the address below. *You don't even need a stamp!*

YES! Please send me 4 free Modern Romance books and a surprise gift. I understand that unless you hear from me, I will receive 6 superb new titles every month for just £2.40 each, postage and packing free. I am under no obligation to purchase any books and may cancel my subscription at any time. The free books and gift will be mine to keep in any case.

P0ZEB

Ms/Mrs/Miss/Mr ....Initials...
BLOCK CAPITALS PLEASE

Surname ....

Address..

....

....Postcode ....

Send this whole page to:
UK: The Reader Service, FREEPOST CN81, Croydon, CR9 3WZ
EIRE: The Reader Service, PO Box 4546, Kilcock, County Kildare (stamp required)

Offer not valid to current Reader Service subscribers to this series. We reserve the right to refuse an application and applicants must be aged 18 years or over. Only one application per household. Terms and prices subject to change without notice. Offer expires 28th February 2001. As a result of this application, you may receive further offers from Harlequin Mills & Boon Limited and other carefully selected companies. If you would prefer not to share in this opportunity please write to The Data Manager at the address above.

Mills & Boon® is a registered trademark owned by Harlequin Mills & Boon Limited.
Modern Romance™ is being used as a trademark.